It's Complicated

Book One
Misconceptions

By

Erika Renee Land

Erika Land

P.O. BOX 49260

Athens, GA 30604

www.erikaRland.com

ISBN 978-0-9852836-0-5

"Life is really simple, but we insist on making it complicated."

--Confucius

Dedicated to

Gizmo 'Caroline' Land

Who lets me rant to her for endless hours and never gives bad advice.

Acknowledgments

Writing this book has been a long journey, and there have been many people who have helped me accomplish publishing this book. While extending an encompassing thank you does not justify the gratitude I have for each of you, to avoid leaving anyone out, I am compelled to write an all-inclusive 'Thank You.'

Family, friends, colleagues, associates, my publishing partners, and the list goes on, I want to thank you for your encouraging words, reads and re-reads, designs, edits, and so much more. Thank you for believing in me and my dreams. Thank you for providing direction for my ideas and spaces for them to flourish, as fly by and random as they were at times. You all know who you are, so please accept this gracious THANK YOU.

To my mother, Renee Rhodes, there are not enough words. Without your love and guidance, Misconceptions may not have happened. Thank you for letting me know that as long as my decisions have merit, there will be light at the end of the tunnel.

I have love for you all.

E.R.L

Misconceptions

Now, everyone has their own point of view, but I want it to be known that I tried to avoid this situation, and that's something Victoria, Camille, and Nadia are just going to have to understand. I never intended to hurt any of them, but things got out of hand before I knew it.

Laila

1

Every Tuesday and Thursday afternoon, Victoria pulls a disappearing act from four to six o'clock. At first, she told me she was taking time for herself, but it's been a few weeks now, and I'm beginning to wonder if she's falling out of love with me. The loneliness I feel when I'm in her presence kills me. I've tried to reach her on many occasions, in thousands of ways; however, she has shut down on me, and I'm tired of trying. I cannot take the twists and turns of this emotional roller coaster anymore. I love Tori with all my heart and we've been through too much for me to abandon this relationship. But she has become so distant, and I'm not able to understand this change between us. Her constant deflecting or plain ignoring my questions is wearing me down. We've gone from what I thought was almost perfect to *What in the hell is going on?*

Those sparks of love I used to feel raining down on us are turning to ash. *But tonight I'm going to get my baby back.*

It's two o'clock, Thursday morning, and tonight will be ours. There's so much to do. I want to make this special, so I will take the day off. I have to get flowers, rent a hotel room, make dinner reservations, and see which theatrical show is in town.

Tori interrupts my thought when she steps into the room naked from the shower. I love her arms, strong but feminine, with just the right amount of definition. Beautiful calves on long legs lead into the roundness of her ass. *Damn, I want her to make love to me right now.*

"What are you smiling about?" she asks.

"Your belly button!"

"What?" She flashes a smile.

"I'm joking. Wanted to make you smile and I did."

"You always do."

"So, Tori, what are you doing later?"

"Nothing. I may get my hair done, but I'm not sure."

Coyly I say, "I was hoping you were going to say me, but since you didn't, I think you should wait until tomorrow and get it done."

"And I think you should let yours grow back. Can you put some lotion on my back, please?"

When Tori turns around, I'm reminded of another of her transgressions. That scar, which is three weeks old, is staring me in my face. The cut on the lower left side of her back has mostly healed, but the scratch marks are still there. Four almost perfectly straight lines, which are now barren of scabs, will always be a reminder of her infidelity. The four marks incurred this time are representative of each time she has cheated. I said I wouldn't stay if she did it again, but here I am trying to get past it, trying to make it work despite my better judgment, again.

Suddenly, a burning sensation fills my chest. I want to ask her about it again, but I know it will lead to an argument. I don't want to argue with her. Things have been tense enough around here. Tori is always jumpy and has bursts of anger she's never had before. I need her to open up so I can fix it, but she has become so guarded and defensive. So, for now, I refrain from asking about the scar and keep my emotions pent up inside. I have to because, after knowing me for eight years, she can read me like a book, and if my voice cracks, I'll be forced to tell her my thoughts. It's just so hard because I want to be with her, but I can't tell if she still loves me.

I confirm she will be home by two-twenty as I watch her dress.

"What time does your flight land in Kansas, Tori?"

"We take off at six, so about seven-forty."

"When will you be back in D.C.?"

"Hopefully around one, if the people whose plane we're taking back don't go berserk."

Lunchtime that's good. "Please be careful. I'm afraid something is going to happen to you one day."

She slightly drops her head and her shoulders slouch. Then she lifts her head back up, turns around, and tells me she'll be extra careful. I've been getting some eerie feelings from her lately, and I don't know why. The last time I felt this way was about three years ago, when I found out she was cheating with that skank co-pilot of hers.

What is wrong with me that I keep trying to hold on to a habitual cheater? She'll never change; I need to stop torturing myself.

Out of habit, while getting dressed, Tori stands by the doors that lead out onto the balcony. When I don't get up with her in the morning, she uses the moonlight, along with the little bit of light coming from the bathroom, to put on her uniform. I personally need just about every light on in the house when I'm getting dressed.

Man, I love watching her; I always have. She is very methodical, but clumsy at times. It's cute. Watching her put on her uniform also makes me wet. It's only been four weeks, but I miss being intimate with her.

* * *

It's two o'clock already?! She'll be home soon. Checklist, checklist, where is my checklist? Oh, let me text her to make sure she's on her way 'cause she likes to make pit stops – What is that noise? The house phone is ringing. *No one ever calls that phone. I don't even know why we have one.*

I answer, "Hello!" then say out loud to myself, "Good. The checklist!"

"What checklist, Laila?" Tori asks.

Ignoring her question I say, "How was the flight? Did you get my souvenir from Kansas, and why did you call the house phone?"

"Slow down. You're, like, all manic and shit. It was the number my phone called. I don't know why you love to text me when you know I'm driving."

"My bad. I was just curious to know when you're going to get here, because I have a surprise for you."

"Well the flight was cool; no issues. Yes, I got your shot glass, and I'm great. I caught a short nap on the plane. Why are you home anyway?"

"I took the day off. Something important came up."

"Did it really, or are you just saying that? " Cause you know your definition of important can be an IKEA sale."

"Now, you know that only happens twice a year, so don't try to play me."

"I wish I had a job I could take off whenever I wanted to," Tori comments.

"Well, you're the one who wanted to play Repo Man, and you know you get off way more days than I do."

"Repo Man, ha ha. Repossessing planes is not the same thing."

"You go in and take back planes that people are no longer paying for, Repo Man!"

"I'm on our street. See you in a minute."

"Okay. Bye."

I feel like a little kid on the first day of school. *Flowers: check. Fruit: check. Outfits: check. Shower on: check.* I swing the door open before she can put the key in the lock, leap into the air, wrap my legs around her waist, and start kissing her. Luckily, she catches me. I only weigh 123 pounds, but I catch her off guard and she stumbles back a little.

I love this woman with all my heart and I need us to be who we were four weeks ago. Lately, in the blink of an eye, she changes up on me. One minute, everything is fine. Then I'll leave the room, come back, and she's mad. Tori doesn't want to talk about much of anything, and when she does, it's with a false demeanor to appease me. But it doesn't work. I can see right through her forced perkiness and fake smile.

"Whoa Laila! You missed me, huh?" Tori says as she puts me down.

"I did, I did. So, where is it?"

"Here woman. It never fails. This is your twenty-third shot glass, and you still get excited."

"What excites me is that you always remember to pick one up. Now, hurry upstairs. The shower is already on, and don't take all day in there like you normally do."

She hurries upstairs as I put her things away. I take the money out of the hidden compartment of her duffle bag and write up the deposit slip. This time I find ten thousand dollars.

Man, I love her job. It's not steady, but being paid this amount for a couple hours of work is amazing. Makes me want to change professions.

I repack her extra set of clothing, reading materials, and iPod before going into the kitchen to get replacement snacks. I close the bag and place it back in its resting place by the front door, because she never knows when they will call with an unexpected repo. Plane repossessions do not occur as often as car repossessions and can be much more dangerous, which is why she gets paid per job on the same day a job is completed.

I really should have gotten into that profession.

I head upstairs as she's getting out of the shower and make it to the bathroom just in time to wrap a towel around her. I kiss her on the neck and she moans softly. She hasn't let me get this close to her in weeks. As I place kisses all over her body I slowly dry her off. Moans have turned into her telling me how much she loves me and that it feels good. I motion for her to open her legs so I can dry between them. Before she can object, I slide two of my fingers inside her. She releases a stronger moan and grabs the side of the sink.

Finally, we can make love.

I begin slowing sliding my fingers in and out of her, increasing the speed as she becomes wetter. I say to her, "For a so-called stud, you really love this, huh?" It's a phrase I've said thousands of times, but this time, her eyes pop open and she tells me to stop while pushing my hand away. The look in her eyes tells me she is serious, I back off.

I'm so confused. The mixed signals are killing me softly, and she doesn't even know it. I hug and tell her I'm sorry. She assures me that it's okay, that I didn't do anything wrong, and that I shouldn't be upset about it. I try not to show my hurt. She keeps rejecting me, and I don't know what to do.

I plead with her to tell me what's wrong, and lo and behold, she gives me the response I knew was coming, the same words I've been hearing for three weeks.

"I promise I'll tell you everything, but for now, let it go."

My agitation spills out. "Let it go? That's the only thing I've been hearing you say lately."

"I know, babe, but I just don't want to talk about it right now."

"Oh, no! You're going to talk about it! Are you cheating on me?"

One, two. Relax, don't blow it. Buckle my shoe. Chill. Tonight is almost here. Three, four.

"WHAT?! Are you serious? Why must you always jump to that conclusion, Laila?"

"Well, are you Victoria?" I ask making sure to stress her government name.

She starts fumbling around the room, putting her clothes on.

"Anyway, what time is it? I have to go," she says.

"No, Tori! You're always leaving."

"I have to go. Why are you always hassling me?"

"Hassling you?! Did you just say that? I'm practically your wife. I can ask you questions."

She storms downstairs, and I am right on her heels. I change my tone of voice and beg her not to leave. She is searching for her keys, which I moved from their normal place while she was in the shower.

"I don't want you to leave. Let's spend the rest of the day together and forget all our troubles. Baby Please?"

She looks at me with glassy eyes and insists she has to go. Lately, all she does is leave. We barely talk about anything of substance, and when I try to have an extended conversation with her, she gets upset or shuts down. Honestly, I think she's been a bit depressed ever since that sparring match.

"Laila, where are my keys? I know I put them on the hook."

"It doesn't matter. Stay with me, baby; we need to fix this."

"This is not the right time!" she exclaims, while frantically searching each room. She sees me pick them up in the kitchen and raises her voice. "Give me my keys!"

I yell back, "No. Stay here with me."

"I don't have time for this. I'll see you when I come back."

"It's really unnecessary for you to be yelling at me right now."

"Fuck Laila, give me the damn keys."

"No, Tori. You're not taking the car that I bought for you."

Before I know it, she dashes across the kitchen, grabs my keys, and says, "Okay, I'll take the car I bought for you."

She runs out the door, goes through the garage, and jumps into my car before I can respond. It takes me a minute to react because I'm in total disbelief that she ran out on me.

Normally, I would just sit in the house pissed off, waiting for her to come back, but not today. It's time for a change.

Too many times I have not questioned her whereabouts, and too many times it has come back to bite me in the ass. I go into the garage and see her sitting in the car with her head in her hands. She pulls off when she sees me looking at her. I follow her, something I only find myself doing when I think she is cheating on me.

I just can't wrap my head around what is going on. I mean I know I've been absent in our relationship before, but that was during times when work was overly demanding, but this time, I haven't done anything. We've been fine for almost a year now. If I can just get her to stay and talk to me so we can work out the problem.

I decide to take my old car instead of her truck. The garage is extremely cold. I need to let my '96 Honda warm up, but I don't have time for that. For the beginning of fall, it's a chilly day.

Maybe the weather is depressing her.

Maryland weather can be tricky. It has been fluctuating between being warm and cold. The leaves have already turned and will soon fall from their branches.

I hope it's not going to be an extremely rough winter.

I turn out of the cul-de-sac just in time to see her turn right onto Route 301. I get caught at a light as she makes a U-turn.

"Damn, damn, damn!" I say out loud. *I hope she doesn't go back to the house. The one day I decide to catch her in the act, she decides to go back home. Ain't that a...*

People blowing their horns at me break my thoughts. The light turned green while I'm looking in the rearview mirror. In the side view mirror, I see her turn into the parking lot beside the 7-Eleven where my dermatologist works. My mind is racing a mile a minute. *Is she sleeping with my dermatologist? Could I be so naïve? Okay, get it together. You need solid evidence.*

I park in the 7-Eleven parking lot and walk over to the next building. Just as I round the corner, I see her hugging a chick who is too short to be Dr. Little. I stop where I am and snap a picture of them with my cell phone.

Ugh, she has me out here playing I-Spy and shit. I squint my eyes and think to myself, *Who is that? I wish I could see her face.*

Just then, the girl turns around and gets into my car.

Is that the secretary? What the... She's cheating on me with that? Ugh! I can't even describe her. Do I make Tori so unhappy that she has to be this disrespectful and let someone else get into my car?

My heart skips a beat, and I feel a tear roll down my cheek. Everything in me begins to hurt. My temples are throbbing so much that I can hear the blood pulsating through them. It feels like someone has kicked me in the stomach, and my heart feels like it wants to seize. The tightening in my chest causes me to slowly slide down the brick wall I've been using to hold myself up. The cold bricks are pulling my shirt up, causing my exposed back to scrape against them. It hurts, but not as much as my broken heart. By the time my legs are folded and I'm seated on the ground, the tears are full-fledged. I pull my legs to my chest, wrap my arms around them, grab my elbows, and cry. *It's all too much. I've given her everything, and all I get in return is heartache.*

In an attempt to pull it together, I thrust my head back and scream as it hits the wall. The pain is excruciating. My hair is cut into a fade, so I don't have any cushion between the wall and my scalp. The pain makes me cry harder. I'm probably going to develop a knot. I struggle to pull myself up the brick wall. Once I do, I slowly walk back to my car.

My mind is shifting too much between anger and sadness. I erratically drive home, planning to have a 'Waiting to Exhale' moment with her stuff, but by the time I walk through the front door, my anger has subsided and sorrow has set in. My legs feel like Jell-O, and all I can do is collapse on the floor. *Why is this happening to me again, to us again? What am I doing wrong? I need to call my best friend Trey. That's what I need to do. He always knows how to make me feel better and how to talk some sense into me.*

"Hey Trey. It's Laila. I think Tori is cheating on me again. Call me back. I need you."

Hours later, I come to my senses and decide to not take this anymore.

I will not sit and cry. I'm not even going to say anything to her. From this moment on, I'm going to take care of me. Fuck her and the damn secretary! I'm Laila Morriston, thirty-two-year-old Landscape Architect of the Year. Shoot, one of the best environmental civil engineers in the country, and I don't need this shit.

2

I was hoping Tori would've been home by now. She's not answering her phone, and it's eleven-thirty. Trey hasn't called me back, and these walls, lined with the pictures of Tori and I when we were happy, are driving me crazy.

I need to get out of here and stop waiting around like a fool. If she isn't back in five minutes, I'm out.

At eleven forty-five, I try calling her one last time before I leave, but she still doesn't answer.

I take the Honda, the only faithful thing in my life, instead of her truck, and besides I really don't like driving her truck, it's too bulky.

I stop at the gas station to fill up. When I don't have a destination in mind I tend to drive around in circles. While inside the gas station, I see two guys walking around the parking lot. I get nervous when they approach my car.

What the hell are they doing?

They place a flier under the wiper blade and move on. I hate when people place random stuff on my car, but I never say anything because people are crazy these days.

I wait for them to leave the parking lot before I go outside. I see they've placed a black flier with two naked women splashed across it on my windshield. It describes Thursday night's special as free admission and one drink on the house.

I haven't been to a strip club in ages, might be the perfect place to blow off some steam.

I get into the car and call Victoria again. This time, she forwards me to voicemail.

* * *

"What? I can't hear you over the music."

"What's your name? I haven't seen you in here before."

I reply, "Robin, And that's because I don't come here often."

Why did I just lie about my name? I'll probably never see her again.

"Are you here alone?"

"Possibly."

The stripper smiles, "I'm Katana. Would you like a dance?"

"I don't think—"

She cuts me off. "Okay, just let me know when you're ready."

The music breaks, and the DJ announces over the loudspeaker that Katana will be dancing next. Katana grabs my hand as she stands up. She then bends over, putting her breasts in my face while whispering in my ear that she would really like to give me a dance later. I tense up because I wasn't expecting her to get that close to me.

Relax is what I need to do. I'm always so tense.

Janet Jackson's 'Would You Mind' starts playing. Most of the men in the club migrate toward the stage whistling and clapping as if Janet herself has walked out. Katana bends over, exposing her ass, which I hadn't noticed earlier under the purple and red rotating lights. In fact, before she walked up to me, I hadn't noticed much because I'm so spaced out.

Normally, I survey the decorum and structure of a place as soon as I enter. But this time, I was completely oblivious

23

to the femininity in the air of this place. It's a new establishment on U Street, discreetly blending in with numerous bars, restaurants, and boutiques.

The small sign at the top of the staircase doesn't do the basement establishment any justice once you descend the stairs. After entering the dark-tinted double doors, I was met by a sweet fragrance, not the stale, rank, smokiness I recall from a visit to another strip club a couple years ago. There are dark blue and grey lounge chairs throughout, the colors of Howard University, which is a couple blocks away. The same colors decorate the billiard room that's illuminated by white lights, unlike the rotating neon lights keeping the main room lit. There are two small stages situated diagonally from the bar, creating a triangle. Behind the bar is a glass enclosure with a woman taking a shower under a thin rain showerhead, the same kind I have in my bathroom. On the round and square tables are LED tealight candles that reflect off the women's overly oiled skin.

When I first entered the club and walked over to the bar, Katana was in the shower washing the last of the bubbled soap from her body. When she realized I was watching her, she smiled and winked at me. I turned and walked away.

* * *

On the stage, Katana begins her dance by wiping the silver pole up and down. As the song plays, she proceeds to do the most seductive dance I've ever seen, not that I've seen a lot. She begins by slowly feeling herself up, arousing her nipples, and then slowly sliding her hands down her stomach to between her legs. As she's dancing, her eyes catch mine and invite me to the stage. I want to step forward and tip her, but I am frozen in place, captivated by the way every part of her body screams, "Fuck me." Katana is on all fours, thrusting back and forth, slowly sliding her knees together and then apart, over and over again while rotating her hips in a circular motion. I move toward the stage, and our eyes remain glued. "Would You Mind" fades into the background and "Drop it Low" by Ester Dean starts blaring.

Katana slides into a split and starts bouncing her cheeks to the beat. I'm as wet as a rapid river, and five hundred dollars of Victoria's money is gone by the time Katana leaves the stage. Yes, I took the cash out of Tori's account. I know it was rude of me, but right now I don't care.

Katana is approaching everyone with her mandatory thank yous when our eyes meet again for a third time. It takes everything in me to break the connection and divert my eyes to the floor. She motions for me to come to her, and I almost scream. I want to stand still, but I'm gliding toward her. I can no longer feel the ground beneath my feet, people around me fade away, and silence overwhelms me as I near her. I'm mesmerized. *What's happening to me? Am I really feeling this way in a strip club?*

Katana's beauty is intoxicating me; that's what it is the pheromones in the air.

I wonder what she tastes like.

When I finally reach her, she tells me to get ready for my dance. If I hadn't had three drinks, I would have contested her demand.

I yell over the music, "But I never said I wanted a dance."

"No worries, beautiful. Meet me by the private rooms. I have to go change."

I smirk and say, "So, you like to be in charge of things."

She smiles at my statement, turns around, bends over, smacks her ass, and then says, "Yes."

When she stands upright and walks away, my shirt is clinched between her cheeks and following her.

Inside the room that's barely larger than a coat closet, my hand is between my legs, trying to calm my throbbing. Watching her approach through the black-tinted door, I notice her head is cocked to the side, and she has an enormous smile on her face. I pull my fingers away from my clit. When she enters, she turns off the light.

"Why did you do that?" I ask.

"Because you can see from the outside when the light is on."

"Shit, are you serious?"

Come on, Laila. What are you doing? I should just end this right now and go home, but she is so damn sexy.

"Yes, but relax. You can barely see in here. I don't think anyone saw you touching yourself," she chuckles.

My head drops with embarrassment, and I cover my mouth with my hand.

"It's all right. I've seen worse. Now watch me undress."

She is so commanding. As she undresses, leaving only her thong and pumps on, she tells me that every night she chooses one lucky lady to give a lap dance to, and that I am number two for the night.

"Why are you doing it again?" I ask.

"I couldn't resist myself. You're a cutie."

"Well, you're pretty cute yourself. So, do you like women, Katana, or do you just like to please people?"

Probably just wants to make a buck from whomever she can.

"I do, but no one here knows that. I have an image to keep up."

I try to ask her another question, but she tells me to stop talking as she extends her leg, placing the six-inch heel of her shoe next to my head. She exposes her wet pussy and tells me that she wants to take her thong off, but regulations prevent it. So, instead, she pulls it to the side. I tell her it doesn't matter because you can barely tell she has one on.

The beat of the song drops and so does she. She swiftly pulls her leg down, turns around, and plants her ass on my crotch. My vagina jumps as she rocks back and forth on my lap. I slide my legs further apart just before she flips down, does a headstand, and starts rotating her hips in a circle. *I want her so bad.* She stands up and looks me in the eye before straddling me.

She says to me, "I want you to relax and go with the flow, okay?"

I ask myself, *What is she about to do to me?* But "okay" is all I manage to say.

Katana straddles my legs, puts my hands on her ass, and then slowly sits down before kissing me softly on the neck.

"I want to fuck you until the sun comes up two days from now," she whispers.

This excites me, and I grab her more firmly. The rhythm of her hips speeds up with the song, and she begins to buck into me faster. I put one foot on the door to help her keep her balance. She tells me to pull her into me faster, as she grabs the back of my neck and begins to grind harder. I brace myself by sliding my legs further apart and planting both feet on the floor, then I comply by strengthening my grip on her hips. Her breathing deepens, and she starts cursing and moaning softly. *Is she about to cum? Aw, man, I think she is.*

She screams my fake name, bucks into me hard a couple more times, and then rides me nice and slow until the song ends. My jeans are wet when she stands up.

"I'm sorry. That has never happened before," Katana says softly.

I say, "It's okay. I'm all right."

Wow, did that just happen?

She frantically grabs her clothes and proceeds to leave. But before walking out the door, she turns around with an uncertain look on her face.

"Thank you, Robin. This may be out of line, but would you mind meeting me by the pool tables in five minutes?" She walks away before I can answer. *Is this some kind of game?*

Ten minutes pass, and she hasn't shown up. How crazy am I to think she actually would? I'm in a strip club, for goodness sake. Two minutes later, she appears in a pair of jeans and a -shirt, and asks me if I want to go to Ben's Chili Bowl.

"It's one in the morning."

"They're open 'til two, and it's two minutes away, Robin."

"Okay, you got me. Can we walk, though?" I ask, because I am a bit tipsy.

At Ben's Chili Bowl, I can see her features clearly. Her skin tone is a darker caramel, and she has an exotic look, but she's not drop-dead gorgeous. Her teeth are almost perfectly aligned, and she has short, curly hair. There's a small mole on her left cheek that almost resembles a distorted heart.

My mind is racing a mile a minute. *What am I doing here? I wonder where Tori is and what she's doing with the secretary. Why did Katana ask me to Ben's? Probably because I dropped five hundred dollars on her! Is she a hooker? Ugh, I'm such an idiot! I wonder if Tori will be mad that I took five hundred dollars from her account without telling her first. Stop thinking so much, Laila. Did I really just throw all that money away on a stripper? Eww, I'm out with a stripper. Who does that? OMG, I'm on a... is this a date? OMG, I make six figures, and I'm out in public with a stripper. Really, Laila! I need to go home.*

"So, Robin, what brought you out tonight?"

"Just wanted to have a little fun; been stressed out lately."

"Do you want to talk about it?"

I straighten my posture. "Not really, but I do want to talk about you and that dance."

"Oh, well, we can talk about that later. How about you tell me about yourself in the meantime."

With a smirk on my face, I ask her, "Why don't you want to talk about it?"

She starts blushing and looks down at her clasped fingers. I eye the top of head and realize how much better she looks without the wig. Her chestnut brown hair brings out the color of her dark brown eyes, which slant upwards a bit, and a closer look at that freckle does reveal a heart.

"So... Robin, are you going to tell me about yourself?"

No, I don't even know you! "I'm a simple person, and I don't go to strip clubs often," I reply.

Come on, Laila, there's no need to be rude. You could've come up with something better than that.

"Oh! I see. Well, then... don't you just love this place? They have the best chili ever."

"Honestly, I've never eaten here."

"What? Tell me you're not serious. This is like *the* go-to place for chili in D.C."

"I know, I know. It's always packed, though, and I don't have time to wait when I'm in the area."

We have a bowl of their vegetarian chili and continue the small talk as I become overwhelmed with emotion. My phone has been vibrating non-stop since I turned it back on after leaving the club. I want to answer it, but I can't. I want to teach Tori a lesson. My focus drifts back toward Katana when I feel her foot hit mine.

Oh, my goodness. What was she talking about? I wonder if she can tell I spaced out for a minute.

We decide to walk back to the club after I take a few more bites of my chili. I'm glad we came to eat because I feel sober again.

"Earlier you said you wanted to talk about my dance. I can show you the extended version of the dance, if you like."

Wow, that was really direct! How can I resist her and that million-dollar smile? Ask her if she's a hooker. OMG, what are you doing, Laila? I really need to get home; it's already two o'clock. Don't be like Tori with her one-night stands. It doesn't matter if they were flings. And, no matter how much I try to justify my actions, I'm still cheating.

"No, I can't. I have to—" As my phone vibrates, visions of Tori and the secretary flash before my eyes and stop me mid-sentence. "You know what? I want to see it."

"Are you sure? I don't want to keep you from something or someone."

Here it comes. Not the first lie, but the most important lie.

"There is no one, and there is nothing I have to do."

"Great. So, do you want to follow me to my house, or …?"

"Umm, can I ask you something?"

She smiles and says, "Sure."

"Umm... umm, am I gonna have to pay for my time with you?"

I shouldn't even be asking that question. I need to go home. What if she says yes? Then what, Laila, then what?

She starts laughing hysterically. "What?!"

As I stare at her with a serious look on my face, she shakes her head and says, "No, honey. I strip, but I don't prostitute myself. I'm genuinely attracted to you."

"Oh, okay. Sorry if I offended you. You know, maybe we should…"

"No, it's okay. You didn't."

Come on, Laila, back out. You can do it. No, Tori needs to know what it feels like.

"I have another question."

Still laughing, she gestures for me to ask her.

"Are you a serial killer, rapist, thief, or any type of criminal? Have you ever been convicted of a crime, including misdemeanors?"

She gets serious and squints at me. "Nooo to all of the above. Have you?" Then she laughs again.

I laugh along with her. "No. I'll follow you, if that's okay. Just know I'm stronger than I look, and I have a gun."

She wrinkles her brow. "I bet you are. We don't have to do this if you're nervous."

This is your chance. Take it. I check my phone and read the text from Tori, which says, *"Where the F R U?"* She has the audacity to question me after being gone for almost eight hours.

Mostly out of anger, I make the decision to go with Katana to her house. We walk back to the strip club, and I get into my car while she goes inside. The butterflies settle in when she waves at me just before getting into a Lincoln Mark LT pick-up truck.

She has the same kind of truck as Tori. Ain't that a bitch?

"How about we go to a hotel instead?" I yell from across the parking lot.

"Okay, but only if you allow me to pay for it."

I yell back, "I can't do that. Let's go half."

Am I crazy? Is this really about to happen? I need to go home. What is wrong with me?

She tells me that she has to go home for something first. Normally, these recurring thoughts to run would make me bolt, but tonight, I just don't care. We discuss if I should go get the hotel room and wait for her to meet me there, or if I should follow her. I decide to follow her to her house so we can check-in together. I get out of my car, walk over to hers, and give her my number just in case I get lost.

The drive to Katana's condo in Bethesda is about twenty minutes. Along the way, I start to chicken out and go home, but my curiosity and anger with Victoria keeps me following her.

She invites me into her condo. I panic a little but I've come too far now to back out.

God, Laila, what are you doing? What if she does something to you? Shit, think of a quick way out.

"Are you okay, Robin? You want something to drink?"

"No, I'm good. Hey, can we go take a shower?" I ask to keep control of the situation.

"Sure, just let me —"

I start taking off my clothes, and my actions stop her mid-sentence.

"Okay, let's go then," she continues.

On the way to the shower, she asks me if I go to the doctor regularly, which catches me off guard. I wasn't expecting that question; given this is a one-night stand and all.

I tell her, "Yes, every year." *It's actually twice a year because of Victoria's cheating ass.*

She says, "Cool."

She steps into the shower first, and I follow her. We talk for about two minutes and then sex each other for about four hours.

The next morning, reality slaps me in the face. As I'm saying goodbye to Katana, she tells me to call her Camille. That's when it dawns on me that I didn't even ask for her real name.

3

I open my trunk and smile at how overly prepared and cautious Victoria is. I think about calling her, but guilt stops me. I take the emergency kit that Tori prepared for me out of the trunk and search for the extra set of clothes. While tossing everything out of the bag, I find a note Tori's written me.

It says: *If you are using this kit, remember everything will be okay because your superwoman is on her way. Please don't panic. I'm not that far away. And remember, we have OnStar to save the day. Love, Victoria.*

She is so silly. I wish I could see that side of her instead of the angry woman who's surfaced in the past month.

I briskly walk towards the elevator and call my assistant to tell her to unlock my office. When I get upstairs, Tasha is waiting at the elevator with a mouthful of news and questions.

"Good afternoon, Ms. Morriston."

"Why are you smirking at me, Tasha?"

Her voice drops to a whisper. "Ms. Greer came by about an hour ago looking for you."

"What did she say?"

"That she wanted to surprise you for lunch."

"And what did you tell her?"

"That you were in a meeting."

"And what did she say?"

"She asked me a couple of questions that I had comebacks for. You know how I do."

My heart sinks at the fact that Tasha had to lie to Tori. Lying to Tori is something I rarely do. I should have just gone home. I let myself stoop to her level, and it has done nothing but promote guilty feelings.

Tasha and I walk into my office, and I begin to change clothes once she closes the blinds. These clothes are tighter than I remember. I ask Tasha if she can tell I've gained weight. She replies no and says I look gorgeous. I deflect her statement and sit down to check my email while she tells me about the conversation she had with Tori.

I really like Tasha, so I've faltered in how close I let her get to me. She always has my back, but she gossips so much. She is the best assistant I've had, though. Over the past two years, she has become very in tune with my needs, wants, and expectations.

"Did Tori come into my office?" I ask her.

"No. I told her that I saw you lock the door before you left. I could tell she wanted to, though. Are you two all right, Ms. Morriston? This is not like you."

"What do you mean?"

"I mean, you hardly ever come in late."

"I just got tied up, that's all."

She pauses and then asks me again how Tori and I are doing. Normally, I would indulge her, but not today. Tasha has a thing for gay people. I think she's confused about her sexuality. Every day she tells me she doesn't like women, but I notice her checking me out when she thinks I'm not watching. Early on, I thought she was just intrigued by me, but then I started getting this feeling that she likes me. This is one of the reasons I had to stop letting her take those weekly pictures of me. At first, it was cool. She told me it was for an art class at the community college, but then I found out she wasn't in school anymore. That provided me an excuse to put a stop to it. She told me she planned on going back to school soon, so that's the reason she kept taking the pictures—to complete the portfolio.

"Tasha, you know I tell you a lot of things because there are some things you need to know since you're my assistant, but I want you to leave this one alone."

"Understood, Miss M. understood."

"Do I have any messages?"

"There are a few. I'll go get them. Oh, yeah. Trey has been calling all day."

"Thank you."

When she leaves, I read the email from Tori, which says, *Baby, I am sorry for running out on you. Please come home.*

I delete the email and then send her a text asking her whereabouts. She is in Bowie.

Good. That gives me enough time to make it home and get in the shower.

I grab the messages from Tasha and head for the door. On the way out, my project manager, John Twit, stops me and wants to talk about the Spady account. I get a kick out of his last name. Twit fits his personality. He's always running around trying to find a sticky note or something else he's lost. He also has a quirky sense of humor. John is absolutely brilliant when it comes to topography maps, though. He awes me every time he transforms a 2D picture into a contour model.

"Have you finished the drafts for the Spady Ranch?" John asks.

"I haven't. They're almost done, though."

"Can you email them to me by Tuesday?"

"I'll have it done by Monday, but right now I'm going through some personal things, so I have to go."

Then he says, "I can tell."

He can tell? What does that mean? He gets on my nerves sometimes!

"Listen, John, can you email me your questions, please?"

"But I need to talk to you now, Ms. Morriston." He uses my last name when he really wants to get my attention.

"Okay, John, what is it?"

He looks past my shoulder, so I look behind me to see what he's looking at. It's Tasha.

"Listen, Laila," he starts whispering, "I want you to take next week off. When you come back, you will have a new assistant."

"What are you talking about? How come no one said anything sooner? John, what's going on?"

"The Bleakes want to do some personnel reassignments, and you're not the only one who will be getting a new assistant."

"Why? I don't want a new assistant. Tasha is great, and I've taken to her." John is lying to me. His lip twitches and he starts adjusting his glasses a lot when he's lying.

"Well, she sure has taken to you."

He's such a smart aleck. Breathe, Laila. Breathe.

"Huh? What are you talking about?"

"Look, don't worry about it. Take the week to de-stress, and I'll see you when you get back."

"De-stress?! John, I'm not in the mood for this. What are you trying to insinuate?"

"Nothing. Just go home and rest. Everything will be taken care of."

Ugh, I don't have time for this shit.

I tell John to email me again as I walk away. I have to make it home before Tori. The drive from downtown D.C. to Upper Marlboro, Maryland, is horrendous. I'm forced to go the long way home because Suitland Parkway is blocked off. I hate when they shut down half the city because the president is on the move. I understand why, but it's so inconvenient.

What was I thinking last night not going home at all? I need to pull it together.

I call my best friend, Trey, and he picks up on the first ring.

"Girl, where've you been? I've been blowin' yo' phone up. What's goin' on?"

I immediately start crying. "Honey, I fucked up bad. I mean really, really bad."

"What happened, Laila? And start from the beginning." He always likes for me to start a story from the very beginning. He says I like to leave out important details.

"Well... you know how Tori has been disappearing on me lately, and every time I try to talk to her, she completely blows me off. Well, now I know why. I followed her yesterday and saw another woman get into my car with her."

"OMG, are you serious?"

"Yes, and I haven't told you this, but things have been really bad between us lately. Remember how I told you we have sex just about every day? Well, we haven't in almost a month."

"Baby, that's got to be horrible for you 'cause you know you're like a borderline sex addict."

Borderline sex addict. He thinks it's funny to call me that ever since I told him I was thinking about becoming a sex therapist while attending George Washington University. I still don't know how he equated the two.

I laugh at him. "Stop trying to make me laugh right now. This is serious, Trey."

"Okay, okay, I'm sorry. So, what did you do after that?"

"Well, I took a couple of pictures, then went back home."

"Hold up. You saw another woman get in yo' car and you went home? Shit, I don't know how you lesbians do it.

37

If I'd seen someone get into Matt's car, all hell woulda broke loose. Know what I'm sayin'?"

Now that would be a sight—Trey swinging his arms like windmills trying to hit someone.

"I didn't want Tori to know I was following her, so I hid behind the building."

"Bump that, honey. It couldn't have been me. Anyway, what time did she come home?"

"I don't know. I spent the night with this woman."

I hear him gasp through the phone. "Hold on! Pump the brakes! You did what, Laila Morriston?"

Through sobs, I relay to my best friend, "I was so angry that I went to a strip club and met this stripper. Then we had chili and went back to her place. And... and I was gonna stop, but then images of Tori and the secretary... I don't know... I fucked up royally is what I did. I have to fix it."

"Oh, hell no! Did you say a stripper? Tell me you did not just say a stripper."

"Treeeyyy," I say, placing my head on the steering wheel.

"Honey, I'm so sorry I didn't answer the phone. You've never done anything like this before. I... I... don't know what to say."

"There's not much to say. I've stooped to her level. It was reckless, I know."

"No, woman. It was more than reckless. Look, meet me for coffee at Largo Towne Center so we can figure this out. Okay?"

"Okay, but I'm on my way home right now. I'll call you in a bit."

"It's gonna be okay, Laila. I'm here for you."

When I pull into the cul-de-sac in front of my house, tears are streaming uncontrollably down my face. To my surprise, I see Tori sitting on the porch barefoot wearing basketball shorts and an A-shirt.

How did she get home so fast?

She's sitting the same way she was when she left to go pick up the secretary, with her head in her hands. I want to turn around and drive away, but I can't always run away from my problems. She stands up, and I see her red and white boxers hanging out over the waistband of her shorts. Our house is the middle house of the three on the block. The only thing I don't like about the house is that it sits at the top of the cul-de-sac, and you can see into the garage from the cross street.

Tori walks down the driveway, and I stop the car in the middle of the street. "Going through Changes" by Ledisi is softly playing on the radio, and I feel a final tear roll down my cheek. I quickly wipe it away and pull myself together. I can't let her know how upset and hurt I am. Every other time she has cheated on me, I've been too emotional, and she finds a way to play off that. It's too easy for her to manipulate my mood.

She waves me forward, and my heart rate increases as I slowly pull into the driveway. The phone begins to ring, drowning out the words of the song. Katana has called me four times since I left her house.

Oh, my goodness... What was I thinking? I quickly turn off the phone and put it in the glove compartment. As soon as I unlock the car door, Tori opens it. *Man, I sure hope she didn't see that.*

"Where have you been?"

"Pull your shorts up, Tori. It's not attractive."

"Okaaay, but are you all right? Where have you been?" she repeats.

"I don't feel like talking." Victoria tries to hug me, but I push her away. "Don't touch me."

"Why? What's wrong? Why don't you want me to hug you? Did something happen to you?"

"No, I'm fine. Leave me alone."

I walk into a spotless house that smells of Black Raspberry Vanilla. As I walk through the door, I can see my reflection in the hardwood floor. I walk past the staircase to my left and into the family room. I drop my purse on the oversized brown leather sectional and head into the kitchen. On the island, there are six vases, each filled with a dozen roses of a different color. I walk over to the sink, and as I fill a glass with water, tears begin to fall. Wanting to console me, Tori comes over, grabs me around the waist, and tries to pull me backward into her chest. But the moment she touches me, my ears become extremely hot and I push her way. I can't let her touch me too much. Usually when she touches me I'm overcome by this extreme calmness. It's been happening since I first met her, but right now I feel nauseous.

"Relax. What's wrong with you?" she asks.

"Don't tell me to relax, and don't act like you don't know what's wrong. You know I hate that."

"You hate what?"

"Your condescending ways... like I'm stupid or something."

She takes a few steps back and sits on a barstool at the island. When she places her hands on the marble counter, I notice the small black box. I look at it for a minute. Sparks fly from my heels as I bolt up the kitchen stairs that lead to the master bedroom. Before, it was only speculation that she was cheating on me, but that box is confirmation she is cheating. Victoria likes to buy me gifts to apologize when she cheats. I got a blue sapphire turtle pendant when she cheated on me with Shantel, a diamond tennis bracelet for Candace and a two-week vacation to Costa Rica for Mya.

I can't let her see me break down. Stay strong, Laila. She's in the wrong. Don't let her buy, sex, cry, or manipulate her way out of this one.

In the master bathroom, unlit candles, a bottle of Moët champagne, and another vase of flowers sit on the corner of the bathtub. As I wait for the shower to warm up, anger fills me, and in a fit of rage, I knock all of it down.

"You get on my fucking nerves!" I yell at the top of my lungs. I slam the bathroom door and step into the shower. The scorching water stings my back, causing me to scream silently, but I don't care. Maybe it will numb my pain.

When Tori opens the door, I hear her grunt. I guess she noticed the broken glass and scattered flowers.

"Really, Laila?"

I whisper, "Please get out."

"No, you need to talk to me."

"Get out."

"Fine, I'll talk."

I abruptly turn around and bang on the glass shower door. "Just get out!"

She stands her ground, staring at me with pitiful eyes. I lower my voice. "I don't want to talk, Tori."

"Laila..."

"Don't try to talk to me now. I've been trying to talk to you for weeks."

"Just listen—"

I cut her off. "Tori, please just leave. There's no need to try to fix it."

"Baby... I... I... I'm—"

I lose it for a moment. "Sorry as hell is what you are! Now get out!"

Unfortunately, the bottle of shampoo I throw at her hits the door. For a moment, she looks like she's going to lose it on me. Finally, she walks out of the bathroom and leaves me alone with my thoughts.

What am I doing? Are you really going to let eight years go? I need to. She's not happy. That's why she keeps cheating on me. She's probably been sleeping with the secretary for months. Why does she keep cheating on me? What am I not doing for her? Man, do I love her! Those were nice gestures she made. She probably did it to cover

41

her tracks, though. Shoot, I need to cover my tracks. What was I thinking giving my number out? OMG! I slept with a stripper... a stripper!

The sound of the garage door opening startles me.

Why is she leaving? Where is she going? Probably to see that girl. Oh, hell no! She's not going anywhere! I hastily step out of the shower and slip on the mixture of water and shampoo, landing on the broken glass.

FUCK! I begin to cry as I pull myself up.

* * *

I'm standing near the bedroom window when I see Tori pull into the driveway. She gets out of her truck and into my car, then leaves again. I pick the house phone up to call her, but decide against it. Instead, I walk across the bedroom and go through the double doors leading to the balcony. I want to feel the cool breeze against my skin and breathe some fresh air.

While staring into the wooded area, I watch the sun set and realize we aren't that far into autumn, but the cold days don't reflect that. It's been really cold for this time of year, which probably means it's going to snow fiercely this winter. The trees are on track with the season's changes, though. The beautiful red, orange, and yellow leaves have started to sprinkle the ground, but the branches are still full enough to keep the rakes at bay for another couple of weeks.

I get a feeling that someone is watching me so I begin to search beyond the tree line. My eyes land on Johnson's house. I see a dark, slender figure walk away from the window. When I see the person walk away, I go back inside.

I'm startled to see Tori sitting on the bed. I ignore her presence and start packing.

"Where are you going?" she asks.

"I'm going to see my mother. Why do you care?"

"Listen, can you please take a moment to talk to me?"

I stop what I'm doing and fold my arms across my chest. "What is it? I try to talk to you all the time and you either blow me off or choose not to answer. So, that's what I'm going to do now—not talk to you. No, wait. You want to talk? Let's start by you telling me where you went yesterday. Yeah let's start there Tori."

"Laila, come on, love. Can we not start the conversation with that?"

"See? That's what I'm talking about. This is not a one-way street. If you want me to talk then you better start talking first."

"I can't. I want to, but right now, you wouldn't understand."

"You know what, Tori? Just get outta my face. Go back to wherever you just came from."

"Ugh! I went to the gas station." I move toward the door. She stands up, "I'm not going to let you leave."

My agitation level rises. "What do you mean you're not going to let me leave? I'll just run out on you like you did me."

"I'm sorry, but I told you I had to go. Lately, you're always trippin' on me, and it's really pissing me off. You never let things go."

I'm pissing her off? Never let things go, wow? She is off the hook!

My voice drops to a whisper as I ask her if she's cheating on me.

"No! I told you that already. Geesh!"

"Then where have you been disappearing to?" I scream.

For a moment, Tori looks like she's going to have a nervous breakdown. Her eyes fill with tears, and she starts to shake before bolting into the bathroom. I hear her scream, and then the sound of something breaking. When I rush into the bathroom, the mirror is dented where her fist landed. The glass is encircled by the shape of a spider's web. Tori leans over the sink holding her wrist and crying hysterically. A pool of blood is quickly forming.

"Oh my God! Are you all right?"

Tori winces, "I think I broke it."

"What hurts, your wrist or your fingers?"

"The whole thing."

A cold breeze blows into the bathroom. "Come on. Let's go to the emergency room."

I've never seen her cry this hard.

On the way to the hospital no words are spoken between us. Tori leans against the passenger side window with her eyes closed, sobbing. I want to console her, but the words just won't come out. Something is wrong with her, but I don't know what it is. When I alert her that we've arrived at the hospital, she slowly lifts her head and glances around.

Her chest begins to rise and fall rapidly, and her breathing quickens. She protests getting out of the car and insists I take her somewhere else. I tell her this is the closest medical center and that she needs to be seen immediately. Her protests become demanding, and she becomes frantic as she screams for me to take her somewhere else. I try to ask her when she's ever been to South Mary Hospital, but she just keeps screaming that she hates this place. She starts yelling that I need to take her somewhere else before she gets out and walks to another one. She starts to hyperventilate, so I pull out of the parking lot and head to Prince George's Hospital.

* * *

Not many words are spoken as we navigate through our unlit home. The air in the house is heavy. I slowly follow Tori up the stairs, and it feels like there's a weight on my shoulders. With each step I take up the stairs the pain increases, and I feel the tight skin on my hip loosen, reminding me of that hideous fall earlier. I laugh out loud, thinking about how both of us are broken down right now. Tori asks me what I'm laughing at, and I respond with a nothing and shrug my shoulders.

At the top of the stairs, Tori looks into the master bedroom. Grunting, I tell her that we should sleep in the guest bedroom. Without acknowledging my suggestion, she turns right and disappears down the hallway. I head into the master to change my clothes. Tori is knocked out and balled up in the fetal position by the time I enter the guestroom. I climb under the cold, mint green sheets and watch her, the woman I love, have nightmares again.

I wish I knew what's going on in her head.

Her shuddering, whimpering, and jumping make me cry softly. I move closer to her and try to soothe both of us.

"I love you, Tori. I really do, but I will not be able to make it through you cheating on me again. Why can't we fix this? We were doing so well. I don't want to backslide to the way we used to be." My eyes close and I stop speaking out loud.

Can't you just open up and talk to me? What happened, love? What happened for you to act like this? Did I do something? Why am I not good enough? We need to go to a therapist. That's it! We need therapy.

* * *

The sound of that generic cell phone voice startles me awake, alerting me that I have nine new messages. Once I rollover, I see Tori sitting in the burgundy armchair, scribbling on her arm brace.

"Morning."

Her reply is a formal, "Laila."

"What time did you get up?"

45

"About an hour ago... when I realized your phone was vibrating in my pants."

My eyes immediately divert toward the floor. I try to change the conversation.

"How about we go to Baltimore for the day?"

Snidely, she tells me that her wrist hurts too badly and she wants to stay in.

"Is there anything you want to do in the house?"

"I want you to tell me why you tried to hide your phone in the glove box."

I swing my legs over the side of the bed and suck air in through my teeth because my hip is extremely sore.

"Come on, Tori. Let's go shower."

"It's trashed, remember?"

"We have two other bathrooms."

Tori gets up and walks out of the room.

If she walks out on me one more time, I swear to God. I check myself quickly and proceed to follow her out of the room, but when I stand up, I stumble.

Once I make it to the doorway, I yell, "Tori!"

"What?"

"Oh, I thought you went downstairs."

She is standing next to a picture of us in Seattle with Mount Rainier in the background. Her head is tilted back, against the wall and she's holding her arm with the brace. I lean in and hug her; she doesn't let her arm go. She no longer embraces me the way she used to. She flinches all the time, like she finds me repulsive or something. I've had to put up with different stuff over the years, but this is new. I don't know if I can take it. I'm falling apart on the inside, and she doesn't even know it.

I want to tell her how I feel, but the words just won't come out. It's weird because when it comes to everything else in my life, I have it under control. But I get so flustered when it comes to her.

"Tori, please let's go out today and spend some time together. We can go to that state park up the road—Rosary."

Her face is blank as she whispers, "No, I just want to stay in today."

I blurt out, "I can't take this anymore," and walk away from her.

I'm in the bathroom sweeping shards of glass into a pile when she comes in and places my phone on the corner of the sink.

"Who keeps blowing up your phone?"

I'm glad my back is to her, because my expression would have told her I'm about to lie. I delay answering for a couple of seconds to steady my voice.

"What's the number?"

"706-461-2417."

"I don't know... probably someone from work."

"Humph! Well then, you might want to call whoever it is back."

I deflect and ask, "Do you still love me?"

She is silent for too long, I close my eyes. "Yes, Laila. Why do you keep asking that? I wish you weren't so insecure."

"Insecure?! Tori, you don't make me feel secure, so what am I supposed to do?"

"There's nothing I can do for insecurities. You need to figure out how to fix that."

Oh, no the fuck she didn't. I turn around to look at her. She's walks out of the bathroom, but not before blowing out the incense I lit.

I yell, "That was real childish, Tori! How old are you?"

Twenty minutes later, over the bedroom intercom, she tells me she's about to leave and will be right back. I rush into the hallway, lean over the banister, and tell her to wait.

"I want to go with you."

She walks into the foyer where I can see her and tells me I don't need to go.

"Why don't you want me to go, Tori?"

"'Cause I'm comin' right back."

"Well then I'm coming with you."

"There's no need for you to."

"Well, I don't think it's a good idea that you leave me right now. Besides, I thought you wanted to stay in."

She runs her good hand across her head and sighs. "Why do you want to go so bad, huh?"

Tori pulls her phone out of her pocket and reads the screen. Before I can respond, she says she'll only be gone about ten minutes and it would be pointless for me to get dressed.

"I'm going, and that's the end of it," I tell her.

"I don't have time to wait," she says and turns around to leave.

"If you walk out on me, I promise I won't be here when you get back."

"Damn it, Laila. I'll only be gone a couple of minutes. Can you give me that? Ten fucking minutes."

To reiterate my point, I say it again. "I promise I'll be gone."

I'll be damned if she doesn't open the door and walk out.

Is she kidding me? I don't need this in my life. I'm getting too old for this crap. Where is my purse?

Before I leave, I take money out of the safe in the linen closet so she can't track my debit card purchases or whereabouts online.

When I get into my BMW, I find a pink rose in the passenger seat with a note attached to it. Without reading it, I kindly pick it up and throw it out the window onto the pavement of the driveway.

My phone rings as I am driving away. "Hey, Trey."

"Hey, Laila."

"Trey I need to talk to you. Can you meet me now or are you busy?" I ask.

"Now is fine. Anytime and anyplace to get some good gossip."

I laugh, but don't think his comment is funny right now.

"Shut up, boy. See you in about twenty minutes."

"I'll be there."

* * *

Largo Town Center is packed with people shopping. After arriving, it takes me twenty minutes to find somewhere to park. I meet Trey in front of the food plaza. He greets me with a cup of Chai tea and immediately starts talking.

"Ooh, girl, you look like you been through some things."

"Things are bad between Tori and me. Sorry about not meeting you yesterday."

"It's cool. She's still trippin'?"

"Yes, and get this. Today, I was trying to ride with her, to where I don't know, but she left me in the middle of our conversation."

He looks at me disapprovingly. "Did it really happen like that?"

"Well, it was pretty close. But regardless, I'm tired of going back and forth with her, ya know?"

"Is it that bad, Laila? I've never seen you like this, even with her previous cheating."

"I'm just tired of fighting for this relationship. She should be over that 'finding herself' crap."

He reaches across the table and puts his hand on top of mine. "I understand that, but do you really want to give up?"

"I don't, but I'm getting too old for this crap. I mean, I was thinking about kids next year, but she keeps messing

49

up. The other times, there were signs she wasn't happy or I was pushing her away, but this came out of the blue."

"Well, maybe this situation is different and you need to force her to talk to you."

"I've tried, but you know how she gets. And now I'm filled with all this guilt because I slept with another woman."

A tear rolls down my cheek and I quickly wipe it away.

He slides his chair closer to me and puts his arm across my shoulders. "Laila, what were you thinking?"

"I wasn't. I just didn't care. Shantel, Candace, Mya, and the secretary all flashed through my mind, and I said forget it. I feel like she just keeps disrespecting me. She ran out of the house to go meet that girl. Like, what the hell?"

"Calm down, Laila! Let's talk about something else 'cause you raising your voice too much."

"I probably should go anyway. Need to clear my head."

"Are you sure, we just got here?"

"Yeah, I need to think."

"Okay, babe. I'm gonna stay here and see how many down-low brothers I can pick out."

I can't help but laugh at him. "You're so gay. I'll call you soon. Thank you for meeting with me. I love you and stay out of trouble."

"Shoot, you're the one who needs to stay outta trouble."

I try to pull myself together as I walk to the car.

4

The landscaping is always immaculate in front of the Grove Shady Assisted Living facility. The pristine flowers are one, though not the most important, reason I chose this facility for my mother. She has Alzheimer's. I need to visit her more often, but it saddens me to see her deteriorating state. Sometimes she doesn't remember me, her only child and it breaks my heart, and I know that's not really a reason but —

Oh, shit! Damn, did I really just fall? I don't believe this. This is so embarrassing. I don't believe I just tripped and fell into this bed of flowers. I know she saw me hit the dirt. The gorgeous stud I was staring at before I fell is running towards me, and I look a hot mess.

"Whoa Robin, are you okay?"

"Robin? Who…?" As I pick myself up off the ground, I realize who she is.

"Thank you. Katana, right?"

She glances down at the little boy standing beside her and replies with a frown, "Camille, just Camille," then clears her throat.

"Oh, right… Camille. I meant to call you back, but I've been busy. I wasn't trying to avoid you or anything."

Wait a minute. She's a stud. I know I wasn't that tipsy the other night.

"I see. Well, I was calling you because you forgot your ring at my house."

Surprised you didn't pawn it. "Did I? I'm sorry. I've just been stressed out with work lately."

"Well, maybe we can get together for lunch or something."

Don't lead her on. Don't lead her on.

"Yeah, maybe," I respond. "I'll call you later today about the ring."

"Cool... so you know a resident here?"

"Well, my mother lives here, so..."

"Okay, okay. Well, I can let you go get cleaned up."

Damn, that was awkward. This whole thing is awkward.

"Yeah, I guess I should do that. What are you about to do?"

"I'm going to take my son Jeremy here to Dave and Buster's." She puts her arm around the thin lanky pre-teen. He smiles and drops his head in a shy manner.

Wait? She's a stripper, a stud, and a mother? Wow!

"Oh, okay. He has a beautiful smile, just like you."

She blushes, and he presses his head into her side. "Thank you very much."

"Well, you two have fun. I have to go get cleaned up. I'll call you soon."

She replies, "Later today? About the ring, right?"

"Yes."

"Okay. Well, I'll be seeing you then."

I let her leave the parking lot before I go to my car so she can't see what I'm driving.

* * *

I check into the Largo City Marriot and ask Deborah, my favorite hostess, if she can get Mr. Victor to bring some extra towels to my room. I love these two. Every time Expected Architecture has corporate functions, we book this Marriot. When we have our quarterly meetings, I choose to stay at the hotel instead of commuting for the week. I guess secretly it's a way for me to take a break from Tori.

"How long will you be staying with us, Ms. Morriston?"

"A week maybe."

"Will Ms. Greer be joining you?"

"Not this time. Deborah can you do me a favor? When my dry cleaning arrives, can you call me on the room phone to come down?"

"Sure. That not a problem Miss Morriston."

By the time I get to the room, Victor has already put extra towels in the room and the *Do Not Disturb* sign on the door.

Twenty minutes later, I am dead to the world when Deborah knocks on the door with my dry cleaning.

"I'm sorry. I didn't hear the phone ring."

"No worries Ms. Morriston. I needed to stretch my legs anyway."

"What time is it?"

"Three twenty-three."

"Shit. I was supposed to pick my mother up by four."

"Do you think you're gonna make it?"

Solemnly, I say, "No. It's forty-five minutes away from here."

Deborah tells me there's a festival in Baltimore that I should check out instead of staying cooped up in the room. Sulking is not going to do me any good right now, so I take her advice and go to the harbor. I'll go see mom tomorrow, today I need to figure out how to change my situation. My mother always told me, "There's no need to complain about the situation if you're not going to do anything about it."

There's not much going on at the festival, so I've taken residence on one of the benches overlooking the Harbor. For about the last thirty minutes I've been watching this lady in a sports bra and tights run the promenade. It looks like she is watching me, but her sunglasses are hiding her true point of interest. Whenever she is close to passing me, I divert my attention to one of the numerous billboards, but I think she knows. As she gets closer to me, she slows her stride and smiles, but never looks my way.

What is wrong with me? I need to pull it together. I've already cheated on Tori, and here I am thinking about fucking another random woman.

I stand up and walk over to the bus stop ad to take down the number of the therapist, hoping he can recommend someone closer to home.

I bend down to pick up the cup I tossed at the trashcan since it didn't make it in. When I stand back up, the woman I've been watching is standing next to me.

"Whoa! You scared me," I say.

With a big smile on her face, she apologizes. "Sorry, didn't mean to, I just stopped to stretch."

"To stretch? At a trashcan?"

"I mean yeah, it's the perfect place. I can stretch while looking at a beautiful woman."

She pulls a small towel from her tights and wipes the sweat off her face. I don't say anything.

"Well, I just wanted to let you know I think you're beautiful, but I can let you get back to what you were doing."

As she starts backing away to leave, I reply, "No, wait. I think you're beautiful, too."

"I'm Nadia."

I smile and say, "Laila."

She responds, "Nice to meet you, Laila" drawing out the last syllable, trying to solicit my last name.

I respond, "Ditto Naa-di-aa," making her laugh.

She wipes the side of her face with the towel again and removes her sunglasses, "Is it too far of a stretch for us to grab a cooughee?"

"I'm sorry a what?"

She smiles cunningly, tilts her head down a bit, and looks up at me in an overly sincere way. "I'm sorry; I've been working on my accent. A coffee?"

I giggle, "Where are you from?"

"Just outside Philly."

"Oh okay, well I think your accent is cute."

She smiles and stares at me alluringly.

I answer her question, "Sure, why not? I'm not doing anything."

"Great! Umm, let me get a shirt from the car and I'll be right back. You're not going to leave are you?"

"No, I promise I'll be here."

She returns about five minutes later, and we walk across the bridge toward the Power Plant. We go into Barnes and Noble to get some coffee.

"So Nadia, do you run at the harbor often?"

"'bout once a week."

"Oh, okay. I rarely come to the harbor, but someone suggested I come to the art festival."

"Run across anything you like?"

"A little bit, but I was mostly just walking, trying to clear my head."

We grab our coffees from the counter and make our way to the patio tables in front of Hard Rock Café.

"Do you want to talk about it?" she asks.

"Trust me; you don't want to hear about all of that."

"It's okay. Maybe I can help. But I can understand not wanting to talk about your problems with a stranger."

"Yeah, I don't want to be inappropriate."

She takes a sip of her coffee. "Maybe we met for a reason. I've been told I'm a good listener."

"Maybe we did. What made you stop to talk to me anyway?"

"Well, and god I hope I'm not wrong, but because you're a lesbian and I don't have any lesbian friends, so I said why not."

"Wait, so you think I'm a lesbian!"

"Well, you kept watching me soo…"

Embarrassed, I say, "Oh."

"You're not a lesbian are you? I'm sorry."

"No, I am. I just didn't realize you saw me doing that."

"It's okay; I'm a lesbian, too."

"But you don't have any lesbian friends."

"I'm kind of loner."

"So what changed today?"

"I don't know, intuition I guess."

"Intuition about what?"

"That you need a friend as much as I do."

I take a long sip of my coffee and contemplate her suggestion that I need someone.

"Maybe you're right."

"And maybe we can be friends."

I decide to open up to Nadia and tell her about my relationship problems. When I tell her that I'm in a failing relationship, she frowns and listens to my problems, telling me that she is here for me as long as I need.

After we finish talking about my relationship, we continue with small talk about how the ESPN Zone has closed and Phillips Seafood is moving into the old space.

The sun is starting to set, and the breeze from the water is steadily dropping the temperature. The aquarium building has been blocking the wind from blowing on us directly, but it can't help with the overall temperature, so we decide to wrap up our conversation.

Absentmindedly, I hand over my phone to her when she asks if she can put her contact info into it. While she is entering it, she thanks me for having coffee with her and says she had a nice time chatting with me.

I say, "Thank you for your help, and I'll take your advice if Tori is open to it."

She hands me my phone making it a point to grab my hand. "It was my pleasure. Maybe I'll get the chance to see you again."

"Sure. Let's make it soon," I say while slowly pulling my hand away.

"Call me, and we'll work it out."

I smile at her and wave goodbye as she leaves the table.

* * *

After talking with Nadia, I decide to spend only one night at the hotel. I check out at the crack of dawn and head home, hoping everything will go well between Tori and me. I love that woman dearly, but I can't take the pain. The only thing either of us has been doing lately is crying. Shoot, I may dehydrate myself if I keep it up. As soon as I turn onto Route 301, "Understanding" by Xscape comes on the radio. I push the remote to open the garage, and Tori, who's wearing a sports bra and basketball shorts, is inside putting boxes on a shelf. The scar on her back seems to be shining. It's haunting me, but there's nothing I can do about it. She comes to the car and opens my door. My heart softens when she begins to speak. The talk with Nadia has given me a different perspective.

"Laila, I've missed you."

"Missed you too sweetheart, I hate it when we argue."

I'm glad she has a new attitude, because I'm tired of fighting with her.

"I know. I can't take it either, Lai. Go inside and I'll get your bags."

When Tori enters the house, I let go of all my reservations and embrace her. She gives me a long hug and places her head on my shoulder.

After kissing me on the forehead, she says, "Baby, I know I haven't been as transparent as I should be, but trust me when I tell you it's not what you think. In due time, I will tell you everything."

"Why can't you tell me about it now?"

"Because I'm..." she sighs. " Now is not the right time. But, I need you to know you're the only person in the world I'm in love with."

Red flag, red flag. You've heard that before Laila.

She kisses me softly on the cheek and slowly moves to my neck. We stand there and hug for a while before going upstairs to the master bedroom.

We walk into the bathroom, and I notice the mirror is fixed. Tori ask me to take a bath with her, and I agree. As she starts running the water, I grab the bath salts from underneath my side of the double sink. After adding them to the water, I lean against the door to the room that leads to the toilet, and directly across from me, Tori leans against the glass shower door as we wait for the tub to fill. Tori tells me to give her my cell phone then puts the phones on the bed. I watch her as she walks past the twin closets that separate the bathroom from the master bedroom. As she's walking away, I think, *Finally we can have some uninterrupted time together.*

We get into the tub and talk for nearly an hour about random stuff. Even though we barely touch on the core problems of our relationship, it was nice. We were able to have a conversation without blowing up at each other. The doors of communication between us have opened. I try to take the conversation deeper and ask Tori about the changes she's been going through, but all she says is that she's going to fix her attitude and make everything better. All I can do is try to trust her, but the greater part of me feels she's hiding something.

I say, "Tori, I know we've had our ups and downs, but I truly do want us to work."

"Me too love."

"I get that people sometimes fall in and out of love with each other when they are in long-term relationships and sometimes make mistakes, but I need to know if you're cheating."

She leans towards me and replies, "Honey, I love you so much, and no, I'm not cheating on you. I promise."

I gently grab her face and stare into her eyes. I want our souls to connect the way they used to. A tear forms in the corner of my eye, and she wraps her arms around me. I kiss her cheek and run my fingers through her hair. After realizing how much we've pruned, we get out of the tub, dry off, and go lie on the bed.

It's cold in the room, so I ask Tori if she wants to put clothes on.

"I'm okay. I just want to lay here and hold you."

So, that's what we do for a while—lie naked, holding each other for warmth. I want to confess about what I've done, but this isn't the right moment. It seems like an eternity since we've connected, and I want to hold onto this moment for as long as possible.

Tori goes to the bathroom, and while she's in there, her cell phone vibrates. My first instinct is to call her name and let her know, but the little red Laila on my shoulder tells me, *Read the message, Laila. You know you want to.* I open the message from Christina, the secretary, and it says: *Have you told her yet? If not, don't take all day, honey. Waiting for your call.*

When she comes out of the bathroom, I toss her phone to her and say, "What do you need to tell me?"

After reading the message, she says, "Laila, wait. It's not what you think." As I look at her with disdain, and she starts stuttering, "I... I... ugh... Laila, I know it looks bad, but baby—"

"Stop! Just stop. Listen to me carefully. Right now, I am over livid, so I want you to go downstairs so you can put your little story together and I can cool off."

She tries to speak to me, but I stop her and ask her to leave the room.

Tori goes into the other bedroom and closes the door. I decide to get dressed and sneak out with no destination in mind.

Something always comes up to ruin the moment; I can't win for losing.

Given that I've cheated on her, I was willing to give her a reprieve in the situation, but she flat-out lied to me. There's nothing she can say to explain that message.

Maybe we're not supposed to be together. Yes, it's a sign. We finally had a conversation, and it was negated because she is a cheater. Shoot, she has even driven me to cheat.

As I'm pulling onto I-495, my phone vibrates, scaring me. I was expecting it to be Tori, but it's Camille asking when I'm coming to pick up my ring. *Dang, I forgot.*

* * *

I walk toward Camille's front door and realize how dumb I was for coming over here the other night.

We should have just gone to a hotel as planned. Wait... no, I should have carried my butt home. Oh, well, it's water under the bridge now. I'm going to get my stuff and leave as soon as possible.

I remind myself to go get an STD test as I knock on Camille's door. An earthy smell escapes as soon as she answers it.

"Robin. How are you?" Camille asks excitedly.

"I'm fine. Thank you for asking."

"Have a seat; take a load off."

"I really can't stay long. I have to—"

Camille cuts me off, "Go, right? Can't you chill with me just for a little bit?"

She sits down on the couch, and I realize how nice her apartment is. It was dark the other night, so I couldn't tell how well decorated it is. I feel like I've seen this layout somewhere before. The gray, black, and white color palette meshes well with the subtle hints of color throughout the room. I can't tell if everything in here is expensive, or if it's cheap stuff that's put together well.

She must make a killing stripping.

"Come have a seat with me, Robin. The chair won't bite. I might, but the chair won't."

"I bet you will."

Don't entertain her. Don't you do it. That's what gets you messed up.

I join her on the gray L-shaped couch and eye her black, circular rug for a while without saying anything.

"Would you like something to drink, Robin? Water, wine, juice?"

"No, thank you. I really must be g—"

"Wait, wait. Before you finish that statement, I want you to try something," she exclaims, while jumping up from the couch.

She winks at me, and I can't help but oblige. I follow her into the kitchen, and the smell is phenomenal.

"It smells great in here, Camille. What are you cooking?"

"Not cooking, preparing. I made a couple of raw food dishes I was hoping you would try."

OMG, I love raw food. Is she serious right now? Who makes raw food out of the blue? She must be a true vegetarian.

With a slight smile on my face, I agree to taste the dishes but iterate that I have to leave right after.

"Come on, Robin. I can't get an hour of your time? I mean, who doesn't like to eat? Wait... you don't have a problem eating raw food, do you?"

"No, honey, I don't have a problem, and I'll give you one hour, but then I have to go."

"Excellent!"

"Where's your son? I'm sorry. What's his name again?"

"Jeremy is with his father."

"I see. How old is he?"

"Nine. Can I ask how old you are?"

"I'm thirty-two. How about you?"

"Twenty-eight."

A twenty-eight-year-old stripper. Guess she will be doing that for life.

"So, Camille, what did you prepare?"

"I hope you like it. For an appetizer, a tomato fennel soup. Zucchini fettuccine with sesame mango sauce for the entrée and me for dessert."

I take a sip of wine from the glass she places in front of me. She also places a glass of water and a glass of pineapple juice for me to choose from.

"Really, all that sounds great, but I don't think I'll be eating you tonight."

"Well, that's unfortunate. Luckily I have some basil papaya tortes for you to try instead." She gazes into my eyes, my body wants her; I look away.

"I like the red and stainless steel color scheme in the kitchen Camille. I actually like all the color blends I've seen throughout the place. You have a little bit of taste, huh?"

"I'd like to think so. I like to decorate."

"Really?"

"Yes! Is that odd, or do I seem like I wouldn't be into that?"

"Honestly, I wouldn't expect that from —" I pause, with a look of apology on my face.

"A what? Stripper?"

"I'm sorry. I didn't mean anything by it."

"It's cool. I understand."

She places a small soup bowl in front of me and another on the placemat beside me. She starts eyeing me seductively, and I start getting wet. The wine isn't making it any better.

"Hey, Camille, may I use your bathroom?"

She wipes her hands and walks me to the bathroom and tells me I am absolutely beautiful.

"Will you remember how to get back, Robin?"

"I think I can manage."

When she walks away, I can't help but watch her. I let out a soft "humph" and then check myself out in the mirror. I see the reflection of words in the mirror. When I turn around to read them, I see two sentences that wrap around the walls. *Be true to yourself, don't let others dictate who you are* and *remember what is most important in your life.*

I process the sentences for a moment, and then decide to give Tori a call to see what she's doing. Tori has been the most important people in my life for a while now, and I can't let that go.

Guilt overcomes me. I begin to question why I'm at another woman's house and realize it's an escape. I am running, again.

Tori's phone goes to voicemail. I try calling her a few more times. On the fourth call she picks up. I try to whisper without her noticing.

"Baby, what are you doing? I miss you. Sorry I left."

She tells me she can't talk right now, but she'll call me back in a few minutes.

"Baby, I need you. I want to come back home so we can talk."

I hear a faint popping in the background, almost like a gun, and she asks me if I can give her two hours.

I raise my voice, "Two hours? Why not right now?"

Camille can hear me on the phone, or maybe she can't, but either way, she asks if I'm all right. I briefly ignore her and listen as Tori tells me she has to go again.

I say, "Fine. I'll see you when I see you" then hang up before she can respond.

I hear Tori yelling for me to wait as I hang up the phone. I look in the mirror, change my facial expression to a joyous one, and return to the kitchen. On the way back, I contemplate my situation with Tori for a minute, then decide to stay at Camille's and enjoy a delicious meal. Camille has transferred all three dishes to plates, and is seated when I enter the kitchen.

I tell her, "All of this looks wonderful."

"Thank you."

"So what prompted you to make all this? Was it random or what?"

"Well, I wanted something refreshing for dinner, and I was hoping you would actually show up and enjoy it with me."

"Oh, I guess I'm a bit of a flake, huh?"

She laughs. "I didn't say it. You did."

"So, you actually made all of this?"

"Well, you know I can do a lil sumthin sumthin," she says coyly.

"Tooting your own horn huh!"

"Someone's got to, may as well be me."

With each course of the meal, Camille presents me with a different glass of wine to complement the dish. By the time dessert comes, I'm a little more than tipsy.

"Do you want to go into the living room for a little bit, Robin?"

Dammit, she still thinks my name is Robin. Should I tell her? No, because we won't be seeing each other anymore anyway.

"Unfortunately, I have to go, sweetheart."

"Now, you know it wouldn't be responsible of me to let you drive."

Aww, man, I let her set me up.

"I'm okay. I don't live that far." *But I do.* Upper Marlboro is like forty minutes away from Bethesda.

"Just give yourself a few more minutes to sober up."

"I'm okay. I promise. I got this." *All drunken statements.*

"Look, I don't want to have to take your keys," she says matter-of-factly.

"I promise I'm good."

She grabs me by the hand. "Let's just watch this film for a while. Then you can go. Okay?"

"What movie is it?"

"Like Water for Chocolate."

"I've never seen it. Don't be upset if I talk throughout the movie."

"Okay, I won't," she says as she walks toward the entertainment center.

I love her style. She has this sophisticated androgynous look about her. Damnit she is so sexy. The ambiance of her condo coupled with the liquor has me extra horny. *I need to leave right now before I lose my reservations.*

Camille looks at my reflection in the TV screen.

"What are you thinking about, Robin?"

"That I should leave and go home."

"But you're in no condition to drive."

"It'll be okay. I'll call my..." *Shit, don't say driver.*

I finish the sentence with a yawn and close my eyes for a second, hoping to redirect the conversation.

Camille comes over the love seat, "Did you fall asleep on me, Robin?"

"No, I'm awake. Let's watch the movie. What's it about?"

"It's a Spanish love story. Do you want to stay on the couch or lie on the floor?"

"It doesn't matter."

She leaves the room for a moment, and I check my phone for any missed calls, messages, something from Victoria. There are none. Camille returns with a full-sized foam mattress topper, lays it on the floor, and tells me to join her. As soon as I lay down beside her, my libido goes into overdrive. Before any of the funny business starts I let her know I don't want to have sex with her. She laughs and says she's cool with that. We watch the movie for about ten minutes before I start questioning her.

"So, Camille, how long have you been stripping?"

"Eight years or so."

"That's a while. Is it a career for you?"

She wrinkles her forehead, but replies softly, "No, I'm just doing it to further myself along and provide for my son."

I turn my back to her; she scoots forward, pulling me closer.

"I know it sounds cliché, but I don't plan on being a stripper for the rest of my life, Robin."

"Besides stripping, what else do you like to do?"

"I hang out with my son and go to school."

"Really! What are you in school for?"

"It doesn't matter. Just relax and watch the movie."

Lifting myself up, I realize just how tipsy I am. I ask her if she's embarrassed by it. She wrinkles her brow again and tells me no.

"What, are you in cosmetology school? That's respectable. Goodness knows we need stylists in the world."

She shakes her head, and then puts her hand on it. "So, what is it that you do, Ms. Robin?"

"Umm, I'm a sales association... dang, I mean associate." We laugh. *Here I go with the lies again.*

"What kind of sales do you do?"

"It varies."

"How many siblings do you have?"

"None."

She begins to ask me too many questions, so I push her onto her back and slide my hand into her pants.

She grabs at my wrist. "What are you doing?"

"I want to feel you."

"No, you can't. You said you don't want to have sex, so I'm not gonna let that happen."

I turn on my seductive voice, "Come on, sweetie. I know you want it because you're wet." I begin to slide her shirt up with my other hand. I pull my hand out of her pants and put my finger in her mouth. She sucks her wetness off of it and I try to straddle her.

"Come on. Let's sit up. Tell me all about you." I get agitated.

"Well, I don't know what you expect to get out of a drunk person, but I am thirty-two and trying to be happy."

She stands up and asks, "Are you single?"

"Why did you ask that? You already know the answer." *I need to be honest. What is wrong with me?*

"Just making sure the answer didn't change."

"Oh, I see."

"You know I would like to date you, right?"

I sober up quickly. "You don't want to date me. You don't even know me."

"Exactly the point. I want to get to know you, then date you. You know... see where it goes."

"Trust me, sweetheart, you don't want to date me."

"But I do. I think you're a cool woman. A little flaky, but cool," she laughs.

"Ha, ha." I roll over and say her name.

Immediately, she begins, "Listen, before you shoot me down. Let's just try to be friends and see where it goes. Does that work for you?"

I think about it for a moment. There's really no reason we can't be friends, as long as we have boundaries.

"Yes, but not kissing friends. Just platonic friends."

She puts her head down, laughs, and says, "Okay, I can deal with that."

I tell her I've got to go and I start to grab my belongings.

"Are you sure you're sober enough to drive?"

"Yes, I'm okay. Do you want to talk to me during my drive?"

"Oh, no. You need to focus. Send me a text when you make it in."

At the door, she says, "Let me kiss you one last time," and does it before I can respond. She kisses me passionately. I don't push her away. I accept the softness of her lips as she teases me with short darts of her tongue. Just before I reach the point where I will do anything she wants, she pulls back and apologizes for kissing me.

"Yeah ... right. Goodnight, Camille."

As I walk away with my body on fire, she tells me she'll call me soon. I scream *damn, damn, damn!* to myself while thinking of all the things that woman can do with her tongue. It's for the best that we remain only friends, because she could get me in a world of trouble. *On second thought, maybe Camille and I being "just friends" will be too complicated 'cause she tempts me too much.*

When I'm about a block away from where Camille lives, I realize driving is not the thing to do right now. I pull into the nearest gas station and call Tasha. Luckily, she is in the area and available to come pick me up. She tells me she will be here in about ten minutes.

When I get in the car with Tasha she tells me she's glad I called her because I was on her mind. I question her about it. She says she was thinking about how much she loved working for me. We reminisce about some of the good times we've had, then she gets really sad and tells me she misses me terribly and hates that she can't work for me anymore. I try to let her know it will be okay, but she suddenly bursts into a full blown cry. The tears are rolling down her face fast. *OMG, I can't deal with this.*

Tasha says, "I don't know how to deal with this," and starts pleading with me to get her job back, saying she'll be a better employee.

"My hands are tied," I reply. "I didn't have anything to do with the situation."

I tell her to pull over so she can pull herself together. Once we pull over, she tells me she doesn't know what she's going to do if she can't work for me. She says I balance her out, keep her in a good place. Her statements are really throwing me, I tell her I'm going to sleep. *She is way too emotional for me right now.*

5

Instead of sitting around the house twiddling my thumbs or having arguments with Tori, I decide to go into work. I need to get my mind off what's going on with the two of us.

Parking is horrendous in D.C., so I call my driver to pick me up. I love Michael. He is so patient and always arrives on time. Now he and I have a routine worked out. He honks the horn and waits for about fifteen minutes for me to come outside. If I don't, then he comes to the door, because like I said, sometimes I'm a bit distracted in the mornings. So it's weird that the doorbell has rang and it's only seven forty-five, which is normally the time of the honk.

Tori opens the door and calls out, "Yo!"

She then tells me to come downstairs in what I feel is an inappropriate tone, given there's a guest at the door. When I get down there, I shoot Tori a nasty look. Then I see Tasha standing there.

"What are you doing here?"

"I'm your new driver. Since I worked for Expected Architecture before, the new temp agency I'm with assigned me this job."

What in the world?

"Tasha, why were you doing all that crying last night?"

She looks down. "I don't know. Sometimes I get beside myself."

"You've only not worked for Expected for what, forty-eight hours, and you're working for them again? What's going on Tasha?"

"No, the chauffer service is a contracted service not owned by Expected, they get calls on who needs to be picked up and when. We are a corporate taxi service."

I interrupt her. "Do you know what happened to Michael?"

"I'm not sure. Are you ready for work, Ms. M.?" she asks, brushing off my question.

Now, I know she can see I'm not ready. I swear, sometimes I wonder about her.

"I'll be out in about twenty minutes."

"Okay. Do you need me to come help you with anything?"

What in the hell? Get in the car.

"No, I'm all right. Just wait in the car, please."

As I'm walking back up the stairs, I yell at Tori to not say "yo" to me again in her life. I hope this does not turn into a bad day.

On the way to work, I question Tasha about the firm letting her go, and if Expected Architecture knows about her driving me. She tells me the temp agency that furnished workers for Expected Architecture went under, so all of the employees were let go from the firm except for a few select individuals. She also tells me she has been cleared to drive for me.

After twenty minutes of her questioning me about my love life, we finally arrive at the firm. On my way up the elevator, I check my messages. There are none from Tori and two messages from Camille. I'm used to Tori wishing me a good day, but she hasn't been doing that lately. As a matter of fact, she has been in her own world.

71

When I turn the corner, an eagerly awaiting assistant is posted outside my office door.

"Hello, Ms. Morriston. I'm Krystal Scott. It's my pleasure to make your acquaintance."

"How did you know I was coming in today?" I ask.

"Security paged."

"Why?"

"Since there are so many new assistants, we get pages when our bosses show up because most of you have flexible schedules."

"Humph, that is new."

Why do they even have pagers? Who uses those anymore?

"Well, let's go into my office so I can brief you on what I do and do not like, and how you can avoid the latter one."

After my brief, I ask Krystal to set up a meeting with John so I can let him know I won't be taking the week off. Krystal hurries back to my office to tell me John's glad I'm here because he would like for me to meet the person we are developing the horse ranch for.

When I walk into the boardroom, two women are sitting there. One is a woman who looks like she's in her early sixties. She has salt-and-pepper hair, thin-rimmed glasses, and features that tell you, at one point in time she was a bombshell. But, it's the woman beside her I notice first. When she sees me, she instantly smiles and stands to greet me.

"Ms. Laila Morriston, I would like you to meet Mrs. Spady and her assistant, Nadia York," John says gleefully.

"Hello ladies. Nice to meet you. It's an honor to finally put a face to a dream." Mrs. Spady tells me it's great to meet the lady who's designing her dream.

I ask, "Are you pleased with the design plans? I had to change a few aspects and dimensions to make everything harmonious but —"

Mrs. Spady cuts me off. "I did notice them, and they are great. Nadia and I are here today because we would like to move up the construction date. Do you think that's feasible?"

"I do, Mrs. Spady. The plans are almost finished, but there are a few specifics to work out with the utilities. I don't see any reason why we can't have that done by the end of next week. Right, John?"

Mrs. Spady smiles and says, "Excellent. I'm aware this may be a bit of a burden, so I want you to contact my assistant with any questions or anything you need."

Nadia grins super hard, and when I say hard, I mean ear-to-ear hard.

Mrs. Spady adds, "As a matter of fact, Nadia, why don't you check in with Ms. Morriston every couple of days to see if there's anything you can do for her? I mean, if that's not a problem for you, Ms. Morriston."

"No, I'm fine with that, and you all can call me Laila, Mrs. Spady."

"John, I like her."

"She's one of our best. One of the best landscape architects in the country, really."

"Do you mind if she accompanies us to lunch?"

Again, Nadia is smiling like crazy.

"No, not at all. As a matter of fact, Laila, take the rest of the day to work on this project."

Toward the end of lunch, Tori texts me that she has an unexpected flight and should be home around 1 a.m. I excuse myself from the table and call her from the bathroom.

"Tori, we really need to talk when you get home tonight. We need to figure some things out."

"About what, Laila? I don't want to keep going over the same things."

"Me either. That's why we need to come to some kind of consensus."

"Are you actually going to listen to me and not jump to conclusions?"

"I can do that. I've already been trying to give you the benefit of the doubt, but you—"

She says, "Listen, baby, we will talk, but right now I have to go."

"Okay, but don't keep putting me off."

As soon as I tell Tori to have a safe flight and hang up the phone, Nadia comes through the bathroom door.

"Hey, beautiful," Nadia says. "Who would have thought we would be meeting like this?"

"I know. It's like we were fated to meet each other or something."

She smiles and crosses her arms under her breasts. "I know, right?"

"So you're a very rich lady's right-hand woman, huh?"

"Shoot, right and left. I do a bit of everything. So, how about after I get Mrs. Spady home safely, we go out for drinks?"

"Umm, let me check on something first. You look gorgeous, by the way."

"You do, too."

"Lady please. I wasn't even supposed to go in today."

We stand and talk for another two minutes before we leave the bathroom.

When we arrive back at the table, Mrs. Spady has already paid the bill and is ready to leave. I tell them my driver can be there in about thirty minutes, but Mrs. Spady is hearing none of it. She asks—well, pretty much insists— that I go shopping with her and Nadia since I was instructed to work with her for the day. So, that's what we do, and let me tell you, you have no idea how hard it is to turn down Jimmy Choos, Louboutins, Prada, and Gucci all day long, especially at someone else's expense! But I can't cross that line since she's a client of the agency. I already feel bad because I've been having sex with her assistant all day in my head, even when we were at the office.

We drop Mrs. Spady off at about seven forty-five, and then Nadia takes me home. We are vibing so much that I invite her inside for tea. We talk until about ten o'clock about a variety of things, from her love of basketball to ballet. She seems to be a really cool person. Someone I could get to know on a deeper level.

When she leaves, I'm in an exceptionally good mood, and my anticipation for Tori to come home is through the roof. I decide we won't talk tonight, but hopefully tomorrow we'll go out for the day and hash out most of our problems.

After getting out of the shower, I put on a pair of lace thigh-high stockings and one of Tori's white button-up shirts. I button the bottom three buttons, lie across our brown suede sofa, put on a DVD of lesbian erotica, and fight the urge to masturbate. Tori comes home at about twelve-thirty. After saying hello, I ask her if she's tired. She yells no back at me. I call her into the living room as I position myself seductively on the couch. I pull the shirt open so it's barely covering my nipples and pull my feet onto the couch.

Tori is stunned, "Damn babe, you look amazing."

"You think so?"

"Yes. Do you think I don't think so? 'Cause I do."

That was weird.

I say, "Come kiss me."

She leans down to kiss me, but plants one on my forehead instead of my lips.

"Tori, I've missed you. I want you to make love to me right now."

She becomes really nervous. "Baby, you know I just got home, and I'm really tired."

"Well, let me wake you up!"

"Lai, I'm tired."

I want to pressure her, but I know it will be pointless.

Pouting, I say, "Fine." She goes upstairs to take a shower while I unpack her bag.

I thought I wanted to have sex with her, but it's not her I want to be with right now. What is happening to us?

I take everything out of the bag, and there's no money in sight. This is the first time she hasn't gotten paid right after a job.

Maybe because it was last minute.

I go upstairs into the bathroom and ask her how the flight was as I watch her shower. She tells me it was fine, and this time they took back a G4.

Remember to look that up.

"Okay," I say, like I know what kind of plane she's referring to. "Tori, did everything go smoothly?" I ask, while eyeing the bruise on her right shoulder.

"Yes. Why do you ask?"

"Just wondering." There's no need to point the bruise out, she knows it's there, and frankly I don't care.

She turns toward the shower door and looks at me. "Are you okay?"

I take a deep breath, tell myself to let it go, and mumble, "Yes."

"Are you ready for me to make you cum?"

"But you just said you didn't want to, Tori. First you weren't tired, and then you were —"

"I know, but it'll probably be good for us."

To myself I say, *Good for us?* Then I sarcastically say to her, "I think communication would be the best thing, not sex."

She turns off the water and opens the door. Steam billows out into my face. I try to fan it away.

Tori says, "You're right, but I don't want to argue."

"Well, I really want you to talk, so let's do that."

"I want you to engage me, Lai, not you yelling. We have enough one-sided conversations."

"Okay, give me a minute, and I'll be out."

I turn around, leave the bathroom, go sit on the window bench, and look at the patio doors on the opposite side of the room. They seem so far away, even with this massive king-sized bed in the middle of the room. I've always thought our bed was too big, but Tori loves it. We always end up on opposite sides.

The joy I felt after Nadia left is subsiding. Staring around the room and looking at the photos of happier times between Tori and I is making me sad. At this point, I'm ready to walk away, I'm tired of trying.

Tori comes out of the bathroom and leans against the towering bedpost. I ask her if she wants to sit with me. She says she'll sit on the bed.

Tori asks, "Do you want me to just start talking?"

"That'll work."

She closes her eyes. "Well, Laila, I know I've been acting different lately, and my intent has not been to isolate myself from you, but I'm just going through some internal things right now. I want to talk to you, but I don't know what to say or how to say what's going on. I've tried to tell you, but it's hard... really, really hard... and I don't think you'll understand. Shoot, most of the time, you're so — frustrated with me that I don't want to talk. I just want to get away. There have been times when I've tried to talk to you, but you wouldn't listen. All you do is jump to conclusions. You know you do that—conclude without all the facts. It's been a constant issue between us. I get pissed off and want to get away from you, from everything really. Lately, when I'm upset, I want to get destructive, so the best thing for me to do is leave and go calm down."

"What's making you angry, Tori?"

"I don't know. It's hard for me to verbalize what's going on in my head, and right now I can't. I know you don't understand that, but... I don't know how to make you get it. Does that make sense to you?"

"That you don't want me to help you with your problems anymore? No!"

"It's not that. I just... I don't think you'll be able to."

"But you're not even giving me a chance. You're shutting me out."

She sighs loudly and falls backwards onto the bed. "Lai, you can't help. That's what I'm trying to tell you. Listen, I just need you to be patient with me."

"I don't know how you can expect that when you're not giving me a reason to be patient."

She sits up quickly with tears in her eyes. "Look, when I get it together for myself, I will talk to you about it, okay? But right now, I can't do this."

"Do what, Tori?"

"Keep talking about this. It's too much."

What in the world is she talking about—it's too much? Is she trying to manipulate me? She said a whole bunch of nothing, then says it's too much. She's a piece of work.

I start rubbing my head. "Tori, this isn't working for me. I—"

"Laila, stop. That's not what you want, and neither do I."

"What? You don't even know what I was going to say."

She sighs and then says, "I have an idea. Can we pause the conversation and get something to eat?"

Did she really just ask that? I've never seen someone be as avoidant as she is. It's two-thirty in the morning. She hardly ever eats in the middle of the night.

Now I'm pissed off. Going out would probably be the best thing for us to do because if we break up, I don't want her to think it's out of anger.

"The only places open are IHOP and Waffle House."

She scrunches up her face and says, "No, I'll get something from downstairs. Do you want anything?"

"No. I'm gonna go to bed."

"Okay. Well, I'll be back shortly. Maybe we can try to cuddle tonight."

I shrug my shoulders at her. "Whatever you like. It's all about you, Tori."

She gets up off the bed, comes over, and hugs me, but I don't unfold my arms to hug her back.

We are so dysfunctional.

6

The next morning, I wake up and prepare breakfast for us. Everything is not okay, but I would like to keep a friendship with Victoria. Love won't let me completely walk away. While she was holding me last night, I realized we need to find a new direction for our relationship.

By the time Tori comes downstairs, I've sliced kiwi, apples, and made banana smoothies. I ask her to cut the watermelon, but when I remember her sprained wrist, I say never mind.

She laughs and says, "Why don't you want me to do it, Love? You think I'm gonna contaminate your stuff with germs from my cast?"

"No!"

Jokingly she says, "You're such a germaphobe. Is there something else you need me to do?"

"No... Yes... I want you to go out with me today."

As soon as I finish the sentence, the doorbell rings and she conveniently walks away without answering.

Tori returns with a package for me from STS Enterprises. I smile and throw the package on the table.

"Who is that from?" she asks.

"One of my clients."

"Why don't you open it?"

I walk past Tori to the fridge. "I'll open it later."

She glances at it. "A client?"

"Yes, a client." I hear a soft *humph* before she redirects the conversation.

"What were you asking me?"

"If there's anything you want to do today?"

"No, not really. I have to go to the doctor today."

"Oh, I thought that was next week."

Remember to check your BlackBerry.

"No, it's today."

"Do you want me to go with you?"

She quickly replies, "No!"

I glance at her with a strange look on my face, and she immediately changes her tone.

"I can go alone. Why don't you go to the spa and we can meet up after that?"

She must think I haven't caught on to her. Why would she be going back so soon? It's only been four days.

I respond, "Umm... because I want to spend the day with you. Look let's plan it for tomorrow?"

"If this brace comes off, I'm gonna wanna take it easy."

"Okay, I can deal with that. What time is your appointment?"

"One."

Now I know the doctor said the appointment was at three-fifteen. I should say something to her, but there's no point in it. Every day she tells me a new lie.

I leave around eleven o'clock because being in the house with Tori is driving me crazy, and my desire to curse her out is increasing.

Since I pulled out of the cul-de-sac, a black Cadillac Escalade has been following me, so I decide to get on the beltway instead of taking Suitland Parkway. Whoever it is keeps straight when I turn to take the Bethesda exit. It must've been my paranoia making me think I was being followed. The person looked a little like Tasha, but they didn't get close enough for me to see who was driving.

After I get off the exit to the spa, I change my mind and get back on the beltway and drive toward Southeast D.C., where I grew up. I drive past the elementary school I attended, Washington Elementary, and make my way to Anacostia Park. I swing on the swings for a bit and reminisce about my mother, Diane. She divorced my father, Jerome Morriston, when I was four and from then on it was she and I, for the most part. She dated, but never for very long. We were one another's world up until high school. When she found out I was a lesbian, it took her awhile to deal with it, but once she realized it wasn't just a phase, she accepted things for what they are.

I really need to go see her, while she still has lucid moments; before her Alzheimer's becomes too advanced.

She did the best she could on a cashier's salary. We were broke, and she wanted more for me, so she always pushed for me to get an education. My mother sacrificed her personal life and overworked herself so I didn't have to feel the effects of being poor. We moved around quite a bit, like whenever the neighborhood got too bad. Southeast D.C. is the area we shifted around mostly, until I was in high school. Then we moved to Northwest D.C.

A child about seven years old draws me from my thoughts by asking if he can use the swing I'm sitting on, because it's his favorite. I say sure and head back to my car.

As soon as I get in the car, Nadia calls me about the Spady account. I update her, and she can tell I'm upset.

"Are you okay, Laila?"

"I'm fine. Just a bit emotional."

"Do you want to talk about it?"

"No, I don't think you can help."

"Well, you'll never know unless you give me the chance to."

"I really don't like to open up about my feelings to people I barely know."

"Well, I think we have crossed that hurdle already."

"There's just something about you, woman."

She asks, "Will you be free around six o' clock?"

"I should, but let me check my calendar, and then I'll let you know for sure."

"Sounds good to me."

I go into work to complete the Spady project plans so I won't have to worry about them anymore. Afterwards, I call to see if Tori wants to meet for dinner, and she tells me that she's sick.

"What's wrong?"

"I don't know, food poisoning maybe. I've been queasy since I left the doctor."

"Okay, I'll be home soon. Do you need me to bring you anything?"

"Ginger ale. I have to go. See you soon."

I text Nadia that I can't make it but to let me know when she's free again. When I arrive home, Victoria looks absolutely pitiful curled up on the couch with an empty bucket in front of her.

"Baby, why didn't you call and let me know you weren't feeling well?"

"I'm okay. One of my friends was in the area, so she brought me some soup."

Dang, she went to someone else before me. That's really bad.

"Well, what time did you get home?"

"Two-thirtyish."

"You've been suffering for over two hours. You should have called me."

"I didn't want to bother you."

Frustration fills me. So, I get up and go to the half bathroom to get a wet paper towel instead of making a smart comment to her.

From the bathroom, I yell, "What did he say?"

"Who?"

83

"The doctor."

Her voice quivers, and she asks for the bucket. I rush over to her and place the paper towel on her forehead.

"Did you tell him you weren't feeling well?" I ask.

"It started after I left."

"Who brought you the food, Love?"

It was an inappropriate time for me to ask, but I couldn't help it. The jealousy spilled out. She doesn't get the chance to answer me because she vomits again. I help her clean herself up, then go change into some sweat pants. While I'm on my way up the stairs, I look over into the kitchen and see a bag from Chick-fil-A, a teddy bear, and what looks like a small card. I try not to dwell on it because I need to focus on her right now, but believe me, I will be checking on that later.

I sit in the recliner across from Tori and watch her, just to make sure nothing extreme happens. I don't want her passing out. I'm going over the ranch plans when Victoria finally falls asleep. Quietly, I make my way to the kitchen, something I've been itching to do since I noticed the card earlier. It says: *I hope you feel better soon. Sorry I can't be there for you more, but everything will work out fine. Call me later.*

There is no name signed on the card, not one on the envelope, not a name in sight. I slide down to the floor and weep silently so I don't wake Tori. Now I'm officially done. I'm going to have to turn myself off emotionally; it's the only thing left to do. I've been through this too many times, and there comes a point when the arguing and lying gets old. I feel like there's no use in bringing it up anymore. I'm either going to deal with it or walk away.

Walking away sounds easy, but we all know it's not. Tori and I have built a life together. We've known each other for eight years and been together for six. We've grown together and molded to each other. It's hard when you care for someone as much as I care for her.

I fell in love with Victoria shortly after she entered flight school. Her energy and charisma balance my laid-back uptightness. She helped bring me out of my shell and helped me see that my career isn't the most important thing in the world.

I spend the rest of the night cleaning, making sure she's okay, and contemplating the situation. I look up at the ceiling and think getting out of this house alone will be a hassle. I love the house, but in all honesty, we didn't need to get a three-level, four-bedroom, three-and-a-half bathroom house, even if we can afford it. And we've spent so much time and money remodeling the basement to make it a separate unit, minus a kitchen, for no reason. Tori decorated it with University of Wisconsin colors, which are cardinal and white. It's a very different space compared to the rest of the house. She wanted a space that reminded her of home. It's filled with mostly stuff her parents sent her and IKEA furniture. She even had the pool table resurfaced with the UW logo.

While I'm in the basement, I call Trey for advice, but his voicemail plays.

"Trey, I found a note from someone. Tori says it's just her friend, but I'm not so sure it's only a friend. I think I want to separate from her. Can you ask Matt if he will sell the house for us? Call me tomorrow, okay. I love you. Goodnight."

* * *

A week has passed since Tori was sick, and things have been going downhill at top speed. Tori is moody all of the time, and honestly, I don't care why anymore. I asked her a couple of times, but she won't say what the problem is, so I'm not going to stress myself out about it.

I went to talk to a lawyer today, and he said I need solid proof that Victoria is cheating, so I've decided to follow her. I wish I didn't have to but what else am I supposed to do? I need to get the proof, just in case she ever tries to deny it in court.

About two hours into the random errand running, she picks up the secretary, and when they embrace, I snap a couple of photos. My heart breaks again at the sight of her and the secretary. I don't follow them to see where they go because it's pointless. I go find a therapist instead.

7

Over the last couple of months, I've been spending more time with Nadia. We get along great and we're attracted to each other, but we've decided it would be best if we remain only friends. As it turns out, she's a really nice, eclectic person. It's funny because she's a lot shyer than she appeared to be during our first couple of encounters. When she's around Mrs. Spady, she's more outspoken and demanding, but when we're in a private space, she becomes nervous and introverted. She goes through a total personality change. It took me awhile to figure it out, but then I realized it's her unfamiliarity with women.

Nadia likes to do all things gay with me, like go to the gay bookstores, seminars, and parties. I think because she has never been with a woman, she is trying to immerse herself, and I don't mind, because I'm getting back in touch with the lesbian scene.

Currently, we're on our way to a strip club, but not just any strip club. She insisted on going to the one where Camille works, it is the hottest underground strip club in D.C. so I don't fault her, I just wish she had chosen a different one. On the drive I try to talk her out of it, but I already agreed to go to whichever one she chose.

When we get inside, I'm relieved Camille isn't working. We spend about two hours in the club, and after Nadia's fourth drink, we decide to call it a night.

I drive Nadia back to her apartment and she catches me off guard when she comes on to me. Now, I was already horny from watching the strippers, so when she pushes me against the door and bites me on the neck, I let it go on longer than it should.

She grabs both of my wrists and pins them above my head against the door. She works her way from my neck to my mouth and slides my legs open with one of hers. She gently presses her knee into my crotch, and I slink downward onto it, she's about two inches shorter than I am. My heart is racing because I know, for one, that I should not be doing this; for two, we are in the hallway; and for three, this is a really big turn-on. She lets go of one of my wrists, slides her hand down my neck, and grabs one of my breasts. I moan at the firmness of her grip. Bruno, her dog, a mastiff, starts barking like crazy, startling both of us and causing all action to cease.

She asks, "Do you want to come in?"

"No, I think I'll go ahead and head home."

"Come in, Laila, just for a minute."

"No, I better not."

"Are you sure? Are you still tipsy?"

"I'm fine."

I can't blame it on the alcohol this time.

As I'm walking away she says, "I'll call you in the morning."

"Okay. I'll text you when I get home."

When I arrive home at one o'clock, Tori's getting ready for work and an argument ensues, as usual. *Here we go with this shit.*

"Where have you been, Laila? I've been calling and texting you all night!"

"With Nadia."

She sucks air in through her teeth and throws her hands up and sarcastically says, "With Nadia. Are you fucking her?"

"No, are you?"

Okay, that was unnecessary. Don't piss her off more.

"Y'all sure are spending a lot of time together."

And you and the secretary aren't? Hypocrite. I swear.

"Tori just stop it. We aren't spending that much time together, and most of the time when we see each other, it's work-related."

"Right, right. Just like I'm supposed to believe STS Enterprises, a.k.a. Nadia, sent you a fifteen-hundred-dollar suit just because they like you."

"For your information, Nadia does work for STS, and yes, her boss does like me."

"Are you fucking her boss?"

This woman.

I walk away from her and go upstairs. As I'm undressing to get into the shower she walks over and smells me.

"Whoa! Are you serious right now? Did you just sniff me?"

One, two, buckle my shoe. I need to calm down. Three, four. I swear if I don't get her out of here in the next five minutes, all hell might break loose.

"Well, you smell like smoke and perfume. What the fuck were you doing?"

"Don't you even stand there like you care, because we both know you don't Tori. You've been in your own little world lately, and you seem to only bother with me when... oh, wait... never."

"That's not true, Laila, and you know it. I've been trying, and you keep shutting me down."

"Are you cheating on me? You are still disappearing on Tuesdays and Thursdays. You don't work out anymore; I can tell 'cause you're gaining weight. Yet you seem to get ghost during your usual workout hours. You've changed your hair. Now, tell me who she is, Tori, or let's end this conversation."

She screams that she is not cheating on me and starts crying, which takes me off guard.

I don't cave saying, "Yeah, okay. Have a safe flight." and step into the shower.

She leaves without replying. Nowadays, this is how we communicate — by arguing. We're either arguing about something petty or not talking at all.

After I take my shower, I call and wake Trey up.

"Hey, sweetie, I'm sorry for calling you so early. Tell Matt I'm sorry, too."

"It's okay. Give me a minute to go downstairs."

"Trey, I think it's really over between us."

"What happened this time?"

"I was out late with Nadia and —"

"Ugh, I told you that you've been spendin' too much time with those other women."

"I know and tonight she kissed me. I wasn't expecting it. She's so timid and reserved, I didn't see it coming."

"Y'all kissed? Laila, you need to stop talkin' to her. I'm tellin' you, it's not going to end well."

"Trey, I'm not even going to try to work it out with Tori anymore. She just got really upset because I came in late, and was trying to put everything on me, like she's perfect. Do you know she actually smelled me?"

He laughs out loud. "What?"

"Yes, smelled me. I told her not to act like she cares because I know she doesn't. That really pissed her off."

"You need to burst her bubble and tell her what you know so y'all can stop walkin' on egg shells around each other. Then decide what you're gonna do."

"At this point, I just don't care. I do me, and she does her."

"Laila, that's not healthy. Why torture yourself?"

"I don't know. I guess I just want her to confess."

"Are you going to confess what you've done? 'Cause at this point, your shit stinks too, Laila Morriston."

"But she started it, even pushed me to —"

"Child, boo. Stop right there. I ain't gonna give you a speech on how two wrongs don't make a right 'cause you too old for that, but just think about this. Something is wrong at the core of this situation that's different from all the other times she cheated on you, and you might want to try to find out wassup before you jump out the window and leave everything behind. And, on that note, I'm going back to sleep so I can get the rest of my beauty sleep."

"Night, sweetie. I'll try to talk to her again, and I'm sorry for waking you."

Six hours later, I call Tasha to pick me up and take me to work. On the way in, she asks me if we can hang out sometime. I gently explain to her that since she's my employee, we can't do that.

"But, Ms. M., we've been friends for some time now."

Child, please, you're just an employee. Here we go with this shit. I just can't catch a break. Ugh! I'm going to have to get a new driver now.

"We have worked together, Tasha. You know how easily people get in trouble for hanging out with their employees."

"So, you don't think we're friends?"

"We are more than co-workers, but I mean... I just don't know how to explain it, Tasha."

"Okay, let's go out for coffee one day and see if we can figure it out."

It's not going to kill me to have one cup of tea.

"Okay, fine. I'll check my schedule."

"I already checked it for you."

"What?"

"I meant: I can check it for you if you want me to."

I don't say anything else for the rest of the ride.

When I arrive at work, it's uneventful until the new interns arrive. We had a staff meeting earlier to give us the ins and outs of the new group. We learned what school they're from, what's expected of the staff we're assigned, and we were instructed to take them out for a little one-on-one time so they'll know what to expect on Monday morning. They attend the top-ranked civil engineering and architecture schools in D.C., the ones we mostly recruit new hires from, so it's expected of us to take extra care of them.

I don't look at my student's bio. All I know is that the student appears to be gay. Of course, they would assign me the person who's presumed to be gay so the student knows their sexuality isn't a problem, and they are able to be themselves while here. I always try to be stern with my interns when I first meet them. This way, they know I'm not a pushover.

I normally let him or her knock three times before answering, then I tell them to enter with little acknowledgement. This time, it didn't go as planned.

When the intern enters, I am looking down at a document and hear a loud gasp. As soon as I lift my head my jaw drops and I immediately stand up. Before me is my temptation, Camille Jerkins-Borders.

"How did you find out where I work?"

"What? I'm interning. What are you doing here, Robin?"

"Close the door and the blinds. No wait! Go grab your stuff."

I call Tasha and ask her how far away from the office she is. She tells me about five minutes.

"Good. Meet me out front ASAP."

Camille returns, and I tell her to walk two steps behind me until we get outside. As soon as we get into the car, I tell Camille that I'm not going to try to pull a power move on her. I can tell she's confused, so I tell her it's not what she thinks.

We stare at each other for about three minutes before she says anything.

"You lied to me for weeks, Robin... Oh, I'm sorry... Ms. Morriston. Why?"

I respond, "I really don't know what to say. There's really nothing to say but sorry."

"You lied for weeks," she repeats.

"I just wasn't in a good place when I met you that night, and then I never came clean about it."

"But you lied for weeks... Wait, let me count... almost three months. No, wait—two. Then you disappeared in December! I was falling for you."

I try to grab her hand, but she pulls it away.

"I'm sorry, Camille. I cared and still do care about you—a lot."

A tear drops from her eye. "I'm so gullible."

"I'm sorry, Camille. I've just been through so much, and, at that time, I wasn't ready for what you wanted."

As I lean over to console her, I notice Tasha watching us in the rearview mirror. I ask Camille if she wants to get out and walk. She does. I tell Tasha to pull over, and we get out in the middle of China Town on H Street. I tell Tasha that I will call her when I'm ready for her to pick us back up. Next, I call Krystal to see if there are any calls I need to return before five o'clock. She tells me no. While hailing a cab for Camille and me, I tell Krystal to have a good weekend.

I'm not calling Tasha to come pick us up. She was being too nosy.

This is the first time I've seen Camille look vulnerable. I give her a hug and tell her to let me explain, but then the thought crosses my mind: *Don't you dare tell her about Tori. She will think you were playing games with her the whole time. At some point, I will have to, though. It's inevitable that she'll find out.*

Instead, I tell her, "Sometimes I get taken advantage of when people find out who I am or what I do. I try to keep it on the low. I mean, I did meet you in a strip club."

"Ugh, don't give me that. You know I don't need anything from you."

"Still, you're a stripper."

"I understand that, but me being a stripper does not define who I am."

"I know that, honey, but I did generalize you as a stripper who claims to be going to school for something significant who really isn't. I mean, really, how could I have known you really are like Diamond from *The Players Club?*"

She gives me an evil look.

"Okay, okay. I'm sorry. That was a bad joke. But, really, why didn't you tell me that you're in architecture school?"

She wipes her nose and says, "Because, as you just proved, you wouldn't have believed me anyway."

"I knew there was something about the design and layout of your apartment."

"It's a Swiss design," she tells me.

"I'm sorry I judged you, sweetie. I am truly sorry."

She becomes agitated, and she's no longer whispering when she says, "Now that you know I actually have potential, your outlook has changed? Typical."

"What? No! Why would you think that?"

Camille says, "Cause your demeanor towards me has changed now that you know I'm not only a stripper. I am so blown away right now. I was on the brink of falling in love with you, and just when I was getting over you, here I am in this fucked-up situation."

I think that's the first time I've heard her curse. Wait... Did she say she was falling in love with me? Oh, boy.

In a condescending tone, she asks me, "What am I supposed to do now, *boss*?"

That's the million-dollar question right there. How am I going to fix this?

"Listen, I know you're upset, but that's totally up to you. Do you want to keep working for me, or do you want a different mentor?"

"At this point, I really don't know."

"Do you have Jeremy this weekend?"

"No, he's with his dad."

"Do you have to work tonight?"

"No."

"Would you mind spending the night with me so we can talk and clear the air?"

She crosses her arms. "At this point, I don't think it's going to hurt any less, Robin."

I send Tori a text telling her I won't be home tonight and that I'm cutting my phone off. I also send the same text to Trey so he won't send out a search party. Then one to Nadia.

8

Okay, so I know it doesn't make sense that Camille said she was falling in love with me after one date and a couple weeks of friendship. So, here's what happened.

After having dinner with Camille that night, we chilled a few more times at her place and then decided to date for a few weeks. Everything between us was phenomenal, except for the fact that I became the biggest liar ever. I realized I was falling for her and distancing myself from Victoria way too much. Victoria was becoming more and more stressed out, and every time I asked her about it, she would go silent on me.

I don't do well with the silent treatment, but I realized one of the main reasons I had to break it off with Camille was because she was filling Victoria's void. Don't get me wrong. We had a blast together, and if I were in a better place emotionally and mentally, I would have tried to be with Camille.

Our personalities mesh so well, but she is a very mysterious person. Maybe that's what attracts me to her. She doesn't like to open up about her childhood at all. Sometimes I wonder if something tragic happened to her. What surprised me the most was that her being a stripper did not bother me much. I don't know if it was because I knew the relationship wasn't going to turn into anything serious, or if I'm okay with dating a stripper. It's funny that her name is Camille, because she's like a chameleon. Outside the strip club, she doesn't bring up being a stripper. She doesn't want anyone to know what she does for a living. She tries her hardest not to be recognized, and without the wig and make-up, she's virtually unrecognizable.

I was hoping all she did was strip, but you never know. I mean, hell, I've been lying to her since day one. She doesn't even know my real name. I mean, well, now she does. To her, I was Robin Fare, a sales representative for whoever would hire me at that moment. She still doesn't know I normally drive a BMW 650i 'cause I made sure I always drove the Honda when I met with her. It's weird because I didn't want her to know how much money I make, but she makes enough money to not only send Jeremy to a private school in Bethesda, but also to attend school herself.

My emotional connection to her was real, however. That is undeniable. I couldn't let her get too close to me, though, because at that point, I was trying to reconcile my feelings for Victoria and shouldn't have been dating anyway. Another problem was that I could tell she wanted to open up to me and she was becoming attached, so I had to pull away before she did or told me something she would later regret. Shoot, I was on the verge of breaking down, telling her all my business, and confessing all my sins. Consequently, after more than a few wonderful weeks, I abruptly ended the relationship just before Christmas by ceasing contact with no explanation. She called me for a couple of days, but eventually gave up.

Christmas was weird for Tori and I. We tried to work it out, but by the time I actually ended it with Camille, the relationship between Tori and I was just too different, too strained. We couldn't find a way to reconnect. Tori and I put so much distance between us that she started sleeping in one of the rooms in the basement, while I stayed on the top floor. I can count the number of times we've had meals together this past month. There were times when Tori would try to question me about where I was spending all my time, but I would tell her not to question me. We now co-exist together, but that's about it. Sometimes she has mood swings that I can't get a handle on, and she cries out of the blue, which is totally new. I've asked her if she's depressed because she's been gaining weight, but she denies it. I let it go.

9

Whenever Camille and I plan on staying at hotels, it never works out that way. The first night I met her, we went to her place to pick something up and never left. Now we've decided to stay at her place for the weekend, and if it will help her feel better, I don't mind. When I met her all those months ago, my intention was not to hurt her. Shoot, I didn't even want to get that close to her, but somehow I got caught up. It's like no matter how hard I try to resist, I find myself relenting to her advances.

I'm sitting on the couch checking my messages when Camille walks into the living room and places a magazine on the table. She tells me to finish checking my messages, then she leaves again. I send Victoria an email telling her I think we need to go to therapy, and if she wants to fix it, she should schedule an appointment and I will be there. Camille enters the room again with a black beanbag chair. She places it in front of the glass table and picks up the magazine.

I ask her, "Do you subscribe to *Landscaper's Retreat?*"

"I used to, but I cancelled it a few years back."

"I get them, but I've only read a few issues."

She picks the magazine up and looks at it. "Out of the ones I've read, this is my favorite issue."

"Really? Why is that?"

I can't believe she's into architecture, and I missed it. Am I that self-absorbed?

"It has an article in it about a young African-American woman who shows great promise in landscape architecture. How she started attending George Washington University at seventeen and got her B.S. and M.S. in civil engineering with a—what was it?—oh, yeah, with a focus in environmental engineering. Then went back and got the Landscape Design Graduate Certificate all before the age of twenty-four. You looked completely different back then compared to the way you do now."

She looks down at page fifty-six of issue ninety-three and then back up at me. I now know exactly which article she's talking about, as she describes how, then, at the age of twenty-four, I had a perm that was cut into a bob with red highlights.

Camille says I look totally different with my fade and that the natural look complements me better. She starts to talk about the article again after looking at me for a moment.

She continues, "I used to read this article often, but I haven't looked at it in years. How long has it been since it was written—eight years? I didn't even recognize you. As a matter of fact, I only thought about the article when I saw your name in my assignment package. I was ecstatic to be working with you. Now I'm confused as hell."

She tosses the magazine onto the table, and it slides off and onto the floor. We both look at it.

In a soft, almost inaudible voice, I tell her, "I'm sorry."

She gripes back, "Well, you should be, but let this be the last time you say it."

I get up and start walking towards her kitchen the way you do when you're familiar with someone and their home, but I stop when I realize what I'm doing.

She chuckles. "Go ahead. Everything is in the same place. Bring me a bottle of water back with you."

In the kitchen, I hear her call my name. "Robin... I mean, Laila... Are you really going to stay with me the entire weekend?"

"Yes. Is that a problem?"

"No. I'm just mentally preparing for it."

I enter the living room and lie on the floor next to her and the beanbag.

"You make it sound like an arduous task, honey."

She sucks air in through her teeth. "Oh, it will be. It's going to be very emotional."

I ask, "Do you not like to be emotional?"

"Not particularly. I know it may seem like it, but I really don't like to show that side of myself."

I want to grab and hold her hand, but instead I place my open palm on top of hers, just in case she decides to pull it away. I feel this need to keep apologizing, but she asked me not to, so I won't.

"Look, Camille, can I try to explain myself?"

"Oh, yes, I want to hear this, but not in here. Let's go to my room."

We get up and walk in opposite directions. I go toward her room as she takes the beanbag back to Jeremy's room. I swing around in her direction when I hear her drop it on the floor.

"Are you okay?" I ask.

"Yes. Just didn't feel like going all the way back there."

She motions for me to go into the bedroom and then slowly follows. I'm leaning on the bedpost when she tells me to take off all my clothes.

"What?"

With a straight face, she repeats it, then she takes off her clothes and pulls a blanket out of the closet. She watches me watching her.

"I promise I'm not trying to have sex with you. I want to do this exercise."

101

Despite her statement that she doesn't want to have sex, I seductively take my clothes off to try to lighten the mood. I let them fall slowly to the floor and make short, soft, erotic sounds to draw attention to myself before I join her on the blanket. She tries not to notice. I crawl over her, placing my breasts against her back and my pelvis against her ass. She notices that.

Quickly, she pulls herself from underneath me and sits cross-legged with her hands in her lap. Before lying on the floor between her and the TV stand, I kiss her on the ear.

"Laila, please."

"Okay, I'm sorry. So, how does the exercise work, Cam?"

She shakes her head. "First off, it's not about sex, okay? We sit here in silence until one of us feels compelled to say what's on our mind. No matter what it is, you must be truthful. No sugar-coating or half-truths, no fabrications, only the absolute truth. Also, you keep your eyes closed while you're talking."

"What? That's scary. What if the other person spazzes out or something?"

"It's a trust, focus, and restraint thing."

"What does the other person do during this?"

"Listen while holding the other person's hand. Wait for her to finish and then ask questions, but only after the person finishes speaking."

She takes my hands and kisses each one, then asks me to sit up. I comply and then close my eyes. We sit for a while before she starts speaking.

"So, Ms. Laila Morriston... Wow, not Robin... Those two months we hung out together were awesome for me. I started to feel something that I have not experienced in a long time. I was allowing some of the barriers I've built over the years to collapse. I thought a couple of things you did were strange, but dammit, I didn't think it was because you were living another life altogether. I thought it was because the stripper thing was bothering you. By the way, I've stopped doing that, but you broke it off with me before I had a chance to tell you."

She takes a long pause, so I take the opportunity to ask her if she has really stopped stripping. *I probably should start the conversation somewhere else, but I'm curious.*

She opens up one eye and looks at me with a weird expression on her face.

"Laila, that's the first thing you have to say? Did I really stop stripping?" She sighs but answers my question. "Yes. I could tell you felt kind of funny about it, and I knew the internship was coming up, so I quit. It's not like I had a lot to lose."

"What are you going to do for money?"

This time she opens both eyes and pulls her hands from mine.

"I'm not stupid, Laila! I know how to save money."

"Honey, I know that. I'm just saying—look at your lifestyle, and tuition is not cheap."

She gets up. "Look, can you let me handle my finances and we get through this?"

"Yes, I'm sorry," I say while dropping my head.

"Okay, give me your hands and start talking."

I close my eyes and try to be honest, but I think I can't be truthful. *It will do more damage if I tell her everything.*

"When I met you, I was going through some tough stuff and wasn't expecting to keep in contact with you after that one night. I wish I could tell you why I didn't tell you the truth after that, but I honestly don't have an answer. It was wrong and cowardly of me to abruptly break it off with you, but I was falling for you and didn't know what to do about it. I wasn't in a good space mentally to be with anyone, so I decided to walk away."

"You could've told me, Laila. I mean, damn, I'm pretty understanding."

I open my eyes and look at her. "Yeah, women always say that. Until they're actually faced with a difficult situation. Come on, Cam, you know how it works."

"But you didn't even give me a chance, Laila. I'm glad it happened when it did, though, because I was about to formally introduce you to Jeremy. And you have absolutely no idea how big a deal that is."

"Sweetie, I am... I don't know what to say. It was phenomenal hanging out with you, though. I haven't had the kind of fun we did in a while. I don't want you to be mad at me forever, but I can understand if you are."

"I won't be. I have to work with you for the next ten weeks."

Oh, boy. Here we go.

"Are you sure? You know it will have to be strictly professional, right? This job is my livelihood and your future."

"I know, Laila. Trust me, I know. I can't believe I didn't recognize you. You're the reason I got divor—" She stops mid-sentence and softly says, "Fuck."

"The reason what, Camille?"

"Nothing."

"You got what?"

"Nothing."

"Camille, talk to me."

"Drop it." She pulls her hands away from mine again, then forces herself to smile.

"You got what, Camille?" I repeat, not letting it go.

She gets up on her knees and pushes me onto my back. As I'm falling backwards, she comes down on top of me.

"I thought you didn't want to have sex," I say.

"Well, you know... I didn't, but you are so sexy."

Her hanging breasts brush against mine, and I tell her to lean lower. I'm glad she wants to have sex instead of talking.

She says, "No, grab my ass and pull me into you." Then she sits up and opens her legs wider, pressing her clit into my pelvic bone.

"You are so hard to resist, Laila. See how wet you get me?"

She anchors herself by putting her hands on my stomach, but I tell her to grab my breasts instead. Then I start rocking her back and forth.

I tell her, "I love how... SHIT!"

She says, "WHAT THE FUCK?"

We are startled out of the moment by a knock at the door.

She bangs her hand on the floor and says, "Come on. You can't be serious. I'm not gonna answer it."

"Cam, go get the door."

"Shhh. No, baby. They'll go away."

I try to lift her off of me. "Babe, go get the door." She tries to kiss me, but I resist.

"Ugh, what time is it anyway?"

"Eleven-fifteen. They're not going away, Cam."

She goes to the door, looks through the peephole, and then runs back to the room with a frantic look on her face. She scrambles to put her clothes on.

"Listen, Laila, please... Please don't come out. Promise me that you won't come out."

"Okay, I won't."

When she answers the door, I hear a man and child's voice, but her room is too far away from the front door for me to hear what they're saying. Twenty minutes later, she comes into the room with me and explains that BJ can't keep Jeremy this weekend. I'm kind of relieved the weekend is cut short because I have a lot of stuff I need to figure out.

10

I really don't want to go home and face Tori, so instead I head to the Marriott to regroup.

I've been seeing a therapist for the past month, and she's helped me pull it together a lot, but I still haven't tried the emotional purging activity she suggested. It's hard to just sit and think about the good and bad of each of my past relationships. She says I need to figure out why I've been so passive-aggressive about Tori's behavior in the past, and why I'm just now giving up when Tori says she wants to fix it. If I didn't know any better, I'd say she seems to want us to stay together. It's like she suggests our problems are not all Tori's fault or something. I mean, all of them aren't, but most of them are. I keep telling Dr. Rivers that I've reached my breaking point, so I'm done. Her favorite response is, "Running is not the answer." But I don't see it as running away. I've had enough, so I'm ready to call it quits. Tori cheated on me four times that I know of, and I won't tolerate it anymore. Apparently, I'm not enough for her, so it's time to move on.

I'm getting way too emotional right now. I need to get out of here.

I call some of my lady friends from work, but all of them are busy. That's how it is when just about all of your friends are in relationships. Sometimes I want to call them and vent about my relationship, but I try not to do that too often because we work together. I could call Trey, but he's a dude and doesn't always understand.

After being restless for about three hours, I decide to take a shower. While in there, my mind is flooded with images of the first time Tori and I made love at this hotel. When the tears start, I get out, go lie down on the bed, and begin the emotional purge.

I am thirty-two, and I've only had three major relationships outside of the one with Tori, and all of them ended badly.

My very first relationship with a girl from the projects that I grew up with in Southeast D.C. Everyone knew she was a "dyke," and all of the out and undercover girls in the neighborhood wanted to be with her.

We all chased after her, trying to catch her attention, but she ignored us for the most part. Honestly, she was a hoe and only bothered with us when she wanted to have sex with someone new. But this didn't stop us 'cause we were all hot in the pants. I lost my virginity to her despite her reputation, and for the better part of a year, I was her sole lover... Or so I think. Then my mother found out about the relationship and moved us to Northwest D.C., like that was going to do anything about my sexuality. Nonetheless, I was forbidden to even think about girls. So, to please my mother, I didn't. After all, it was just the two of us, and she was doing all she could to provide for me so I could live a better life.

My second long-term relationship was with a male, and it lasted for three years. I tried to trick myself into thinking I loved him, and, as a consequence, I put up with a lot of crap. I took him home to meet my mother, and he took me to meet his family. Shortly after I met his family, our problems started. I never told him I was attracted to women, but he sensed something was up with me and his gay sister. Every now and then, he would ask questions about my sexuality, but I would deflect them. I think he's the reason I started that bad habit of deflecting.

Nothing ever happened with his sister, but he was sure I was attracted to her. For a while, things were rocky but tolerable until we started having sex, and it was downhill from there. The first time, I was disconnected and it showed. I tried to fake it, but he knew better. That's when things really took a turn for the worse. To make a long story short, I eventually slept with his sister one time, and the day after I graduated from college I moved out and left a "Dear Clayton" letter.

I ended up becoming very complacent in my relationship with him, and I allowed him to do whatever he wanted to me. As a result, when it came to my third relationship with Nicole, I went into it determined not to put up with any crap. My tolerance level was at one. She was a really sweet person, but I sabotaged that relationship from the go. Poor girl never stood a chance. She genuinely loved me and tried hard to be with me, but I was so overbearing. How she hung in there for a year and a half baffles me. I think I started doing to her what Clayton had done to me. I was not abusive, but I did not trust her, so I questioned her every move. She never gave me a reason not to trust her, but I was broken and she was unaware of it. She was such a lovely woman who would have given me the world, but I was too much to handle. It was hard for her to understand where I was coming from a lot of the time, and I didn't make it easy for her. Eventually she left me, and I have no idea where she is now. Then I met Tori straight off the bus from Wisconsin.

I bumped into her, and her country accent caught me off guard. She was so frightened of the "big city," something she still denies to this day. I didn't even know black people lived in Wisconsin. We started out as friends, and I was her first lover ever; she held onto her virginity until she was twenty-three. I vowed not to be overbearing or too complacent with her, but I guess I couldn't find that middle balance. I love her dearly and I never wanted to ruin it, but it's all gone to shit anyway.

11

There's only so much resisting and fighting I'm capable of. The fact of the matter is that I love Tori, and I need to fix this while we're still on speaking terms. I come up with what I think is a sound plan for reconciliation and call a cab to take me home, but when I arrive, Tori isn't there. As I walk through the door, the home phone's answering machine alerts me that there's one new voicemail. When Tori's parents cannot reach her, they call the house sometimes. They're practically the only ones who call the landline. So, imagine the shock I'm in when I play the message back and hear, *Ms. Greer, this is Detective Mark Cofer. We have some news for you. If you and your friend Christina want to come by the office, I'll be here until four. You can call my cell phone any time.*

The message is from Friday. I play the message five times to make sure I heard it correctly. *Detective Mark Cofer... Your friend Christina.* Then I erase it.

It's two minutes after ten o'clock on a Sunday morning, and Tori isn't at home. Her cell phone is on, so I know she's not in the air.

Where could she be this early? I guess I can't ask that question since I told her I wasn't coming home this weekend.

The message from Detective Cofer is from two days ago, and Tori hasn't answered any of my calls. I would think something is wrong, but the BlackBerry messenger icon says she's read the messages I've sent, but I never receive one back.

Why didn't you think of that before, Laila? Check online to see if she's made any calls. I love how cell phone companies post the calls almost immediately after you make them nowadays. If I was a scandalous person, I would find out what Christina's phone number is, but it's really not that serious. As a matter of fact, I'm not gonna bother with checking anything. I've told her what to do if she wants to fix it.

Tori stumbles in the house around nine o'clock at night, and I'm lying in bed reading a book. She screams when she enters the room.

"Damn it, Laila! You scared me. You and those dang book lights. Turn the light on."

"Why is that, Tori?"

"Why what?"

"Why did I scare you?"

She is nervously walking around the room. "I wasn't expecting you to be home. When did you get back?"

"My car's in the garage. You know what? It doesn't matter. What did you do today? I tried calling you a couple of times."

"I went to Ocean City."

"You did what? I know you did not just say that. I asked you to do that with me a few weeks ago, and you said no. I see that's how we're rolling now. You just blow me off, then go do it later."

"No, Laila, it wasn't like that. Let me explain."

I calm my tone and say, "You know what... It's okay. I shouldn't expect anything different from you."

"Lai..."

"No, there's no need to explain. I'm tired. Goodnight." I turn over and put my back to her.

She sits on the bed next to me and places her hand on my back. "Laila, listen to me before you get mad, okay? I just lied to you. I didn't go to Ocean City. I had some very important business to take care of today that I did not want to explain. I was trying to come up with an alibi, and Ocean City was the first thing that came to mind. I've been in town all weekend."

She must think I'm stupid. Important business she couldn't tell me about?

"Has our relationship disintegrated so much that... Wait, don't answer that. We both know it has. Did you read my email?"

"I got your email, but I think we just need to spend more time together. We need to talk to each other instead of running away or avoiding each other all the time."

"So, you're saying you don't want to go to therapy?"

"I don't think therapy will work for us. You know I don't really get down with head doctors."

"Come on now, Tori, you have got to grow..." I take a breath to calm myself. "I can respect your feelings on that. I'm going to go to sleep now. Can you close the door when you leave?"

"I guess that means we're done talking."

"Yes, and I think we need to start making arrangements. I already talked to Matt and..."

"Stop. Stop right there. I want to work it out, just not in the way you proposed. That's one of our biggest issues. It's always your way or no way."

Don't let her provoke you into an argument.

"It's done. I'm not gonna argue with you about it. Now goodnight."

She walks out of the room without closing the door.

* * *

By the time I wake up, Tori is gone, but she's left breakfast on the counter with a letter.

I'll keep this short, and I'm sorry if your day doesn't go well because of this letter, but I hope it does. I have a repo in Wisconsin, so instead of coming back, I'm going to stay with my parents for a couple of weeks. I think we need some time apart to gather ourselves individually. These past few months have shown that we are unable to co-exist together peacefully. I hate all the arguing we've been doing, but at the moment, there's not much we can do to change it. I'm going through some things that you can't understand, and I don't want to stress you out because you know you don't deal with stress well. Laila, I do and am in love with you, but right now, I'm unable to show you that and be there in the ways you need. I ask that you stay patient with me, and things will get better. At the moment, though, I need some time to myself to figure out how to live again. I will call you when I get settled. I love you.

She left unannounced, and I'm beyond livid right now. I call her phone and scream into her voicemail that I want her to come back and how this is messed up of her. Then, immediately, I call to apologize for being angry with her and ask her to call me when she gets a chance.

I drive myself to work because I don't want to deal with Tasha and her shenanigans this morning. Before making it in, I book a lunch date with Nadia so I will be able to thwart any attempts Camille may try to make later. I'm glad we've finished working on the Spady Ranch plans. Now Nadia and I can hang out without restraints.

As I approach my office, I see Camille standing next to my door straightening her clothes. Her androgynous look turns me on so much. I prefer this current look to the one she had when going to the strip club. Those wigs were the worst.

"Good morning, Ms. Morriston. Did you have a nice weekend?"

"I did. How about you, Cam?"

"It was fun. I took Jeremy to Port Discovery in Baltimore."

We go into my office and talk for a while before I assign Camille the project she has to complete before her internship is over. I won't be as hard on her as I usually am on the interns, and hopefully the next ten weeks will go by smoothly.

This is a very delicate situation. I don't know what I was thinking. I should have assigned her to someone else.

I give her one last opportunity to opt out of working for me, but she declines it.

"Now, Camille, I need to reiterate that we have to keep everything that has happened on the low."

She smirks at me and raises her eyebrows. "I know that, Ms. Morriston. I have a lot riding on this internship."

"What do you mean by that?"

"I need to do well so I can take your job."

I wrinkle my eyebrows and look at her nastily.

She laughs aloud then whispers, "Chill, I'm joking! I just wanted to see what you would do. I have a lot riding on this, so you have nothing to worry about. And let me apologize about this weekend. BJ had something come up. You know how that goes."

"It's cool. Let's get to work so I can finish this stuff before my lunch appointment."

"Do you need me to attend it with you?"

"No. After I leave, you can either take the rest of the day off or hang out here and work on your project."

"I'll let you know. What time do you want me to come back in here?"

"I guess about twelve-fifteen."

She winks at me before leaving to go to the intern's office.

I have a strange feeling I'm going to have to watch her.

* * *

Tasha picks me up late, which never happens, and the car is extremely cold when I get inside. She's become extremely moody since she stopped working for the firm. I never did find out what happened to Michael.

"Tasha, what happened? You're going to make me late."

She doesn't respond.

I ask, "Can you turn the air off? It's freezing in here. Aren't you cold?"

"No. I'm comfortable."

Ugh, what is wrong with her?

"Well, I'm freezing, so can you please adjust it?"

"Sure." She turns the heat on high, then asks me if it's warm enough.

"What is wrong with you? Why are you being bitchy today?"

"Ms. Morriston, please don't use that language with me."

"Well, excuse me Ms. Smith, but as your employer, I don't appreciate your lateness or demeanor this afternoon."

"You seem not to appreciate me at all, Ms. Morriston, since you can't keep your obligations to me."

Snidely, I ask, "What obligations do I have to you, Tasha?"

I send Nadia a text, hoping she'll get it before I reach the restaurant.

"See? You didn't even remember that we're supposed to have our lunch date today."

Shit, she was serious about that. Lunch date?

I scoot forward, reach over the seat, and place my hand on her shoulder.

"Tasha, I'm so sorry. Were we supposed to have tea today? I forgot to put it on my calendar. How about I take you out to dinner on... How about Wednesday?"

In the rearview mirror, I can see the tension ease away from her face.

"It's okay, Laila. I know how busy you are. I mean you have *a lot* going on in your life right now."

I wonder what she means by that.

"So, is Wednesday fine?" I ask.

"Yes. What time?"

As we pull up to the restaurant, I tell her that I'll let her know tomorrow morning.

"Do you want me to park and wait for you to finish, Ms. M.?"

"No, that's okay. I'll text you about twenty minutes before I'm ready. Here's two hundred dollars. Go find something to wear for dinner."

I step inside the door of the restaurant and wait for Tasha to leave. When I'm sure she's gone, I leave and run across the street. When I walk into the café, I see Nadia sitting there reading a book. I quietly walk up to the table and sit down so I don't disturb her too much. She's startled anyway and hurriedly puts the book away.

"So, what is *Living Two Lives* about?"

"Hey, I was unsure if you would find me. DuPont is busy this time of day."

"I know. Sorry about the change of venue, but Tasha, my driver, is acting super strange today, and I didn't want her to see who I'm having lunch with."

"I don't mind. I like just about every place down here. Did she say why she was late picking you up?"

"Not exactly, but I gathered it was because I forgot I made plans to have tea with her today. She's been so obsessed with that lately."

"Do you two hang out often?"

"No, not at all. She's been working for me for about two years, and this will be the first time."

Nadia keeps glancing over my shoulder, then quickly looks down.

"Why do you think she's acting the way she is?"

"Who knows, but let's change the subject. I don't want to spend my afternoon talking about her."

She glances over my shoulder again. "Okay. So, how is work going, beautiful?"

I turn around and look behind me. "Fine. What are you looking at back there?

"Do you see that woman? The waitress?"

"The one with the faux hawk?"

"Yes. I've had a crush on her for a while now."

"Have you ever talked to her?"

"Not about anything other than food. You know I get shy sometimes, so I always clam up whenever she gets near me."

The fact that she has a crush on someone else is really bothering me right now. I can't blame her, though. The waitress is fine. I'm glad she's not waiting on us because then I would be really jealous.

It's getting to me that Nadia keeps watching her, so I excuse myself to go to the bathroom. When I return to the table, she tells me she has to go in a little while so she can make it to Ellicott City in time to meet the florist.

"Are you going to the Spady Ranch?"

"I am. Mrs. Spady let me pick out the flower arrangements for the property, so I need to make sure they're correct."

"Really? That's a big deal! One of the first things people notice when they arrive at a place is the landscaping. It can be a deal-breaker."

"I know. That's why it's imperative I'm there when they arrive, in case I need to make any changes to the order. Thirty thousand flower and tree arrangements is no joke. Hey, I have an idea. How about you go with me? I mean, if you're not busy or anything."

I smile at her. "It'd be my pleasure. Let me call Krystal, though, so she knows what I'm doing if anyone asks."

I send Tasha a message telling her I don't need her to pick me up, and Camille a message telling her to be in the office bright and early tomorrow.

As we're leaving the restaurant, I see the waitress looking at us, but Nadia doesn't notice. I can't control my jealousy. So, for no other reason than it being a power move, I grab Nadia's pinky finger with mine so the waitress can see it. She places her other hand on top of mine and looks at me in surprise. I grab hers back, but then release it when we get outside of the door. Nadia doesn't say anything to me about it; she just smiles. When we get to the garage where Nadia's parked, she pulls the keys for a Bentley out of her purse.

"When did you get a Bentley?"

"This is one of Mrs. Spady's cars. She lets me drive them sometimes."

"Oh, I was about to ask what kind of money she's paying you!"

She laughs. "Do you want to drive it?"

"I do, but I can't…" Before I can finish my sentence, she gets in the passenger seat.

All right then. Let's go.

The ride from DuPont Circle to Ellicott City is a long one. Nadia has already told me a lot about herself, but I didn't know she only came out four years ago, at the age of twenty-nine.

Nadia takes her heels off and then says, "I was going to change at the ranch, but since you're driving, I'm going to do it now. You don't mind, do you, Laila?"

"No, do what you want."

I try not to watch her when she turns around and reaches into the backseat to grab her bag. She bumps my shoulder with her hip, and reflexively, I put my hand on her butt to steady her. When she sits back down, she pulls her skirt up and starts to roll down her stockings.

"Look, Nadia, I'm not going to be able to focus."

"Okay, I'll be quick about it."

"Thank you."

"How's Tori?"

"She left to go back to Wisconsin and told me in a note."

"Is she coming back?"

"I don't know. I haven't talked to her since she left."

"So, this is probably the end of your relationship with her, huh?"

"It's been over for a while now, but I think neither one of us wants to be the first to say it out loud."

I interrupt her changing by grabbing her hand and kissing the back of it. She smiles and takes a deep breath. I have absolutely no idea why I did that.

"Are you okay, Nadia?"

"Yes, it's just... Sometimes you take my breath away."

I say, "Do I? Why is that?"

"Because I like you. I have since that day at the harbor."

"I like you too, Nadia. I realized just how much today at lunch. But you know things have been complicated with me."

"Wow, Laila! I've wanted to hear you say that for so long. I mean, I thought you did, but I wasn't sure."

"I've been trying to deny it."

When I pull up to a stoplight, Nadia leans over and kisses me until the light turns green.

She says, "I've wanted to do that again since the night we went to the strip club."

"Me, too, but I wasn't sure if you... I don't know."

Nadia sits back and continues to change. I put my hand on her leg, and she puts it on her vagina as she slides down in the seat and opens her legs wider. Then she starts unbuttoning her shirt.

"Wait," I say. "Don't take your shirt off. You're really wet."

"Why not?"

"'Cause someone might see."

"No, they won't," she says as she removes it anyway.

I slide her panties to the side and put one of my fingers inside her. She moans while grabbing both of her breasts. She lets go of her reservations for about three minutes, then her hips stop gyrating, and she turns her head to the left so she can look at me. She begins stroking my arm slowly with her fingertips. Her beautiful, hazel eyes are telling me what she will not say out loud. They are whispering, *stop.* I pull my hand from between her legs and place it on her thigh.

"Are you okay?" I ask.

"I am, and you feel wonderful. But..." She pauses.

"But? You can tell me."

"It's kind of embarrassing, I guess."

"What's wrong?"

She looks down at the gearshift.

"I just... I just don't want my first experience with a woman to be in a car. Ya know?"

Shit, damn, fuck, Laila, you idiot. It takes everything in me to keep my jaw from hitting the floor.

"Sweetheart, I am so sorry. I shouldn't have done that. Don't be embarrassed. I'm the embarrassed one."

"Are you upset?" she asks.

"No, not at all. It was insensitive of me not to think about that."

"Relax, okay. I started it. Laila, what do you think about being my first?"

What is up with me always attracting virgins or newbies? Think about this, Laila. Do you really want to do this? This is serious business. You don't know her well enough to know how she will act afterwards.

"I want you to think about it more. Then we can talk about it again when you're not in the mood."

She laughs at me.

"What?" I ask.

"Lady, I'm always in the mood. I stay horny twenty-six out of the twenty-four hours in a day. I was having sex with you at the café, which is funny to me because I don't even know what it's actually like."

I wink at her and say, "Well, if you really want it that bad, you can get it."

She smiles from ear to ear and completes the changing of her clothes. We arrive at the Spady Ranch about thirty minutes later. It's always a pleasure seeing all of your hard work come to life. The flowers Nadia picked out are absolutely gorgeous; Mrs. Spady won't be disappointed. Hopefully, the Pimlico community will generate a lot of money for her and the family. I don't know much about racehorses, but if I had one, I would definitely board it here.

Nadia and I spend most of the afternoon at the compound going over the placement of flowers, bushes, and trees, before heading to the Spady mansion. It took everything in me not to have sex with her in one of the barns.

On the way there, Nadia calls and has a meal specially prepared for me and my vegetarian needs. It's always great seeing Mrs. Spady; she's a wonderful old lady. After dinner, we sit and chat for hours. Ten o'clock seems to roll around in the blink of an eye. Miss Spady has her private helicopter fly me back to D.C. because it's so late. As I'm looking out the chopper window, lights illuminating manicured bushes catch my eye. The bushes are cut to read Jerkins-Borders. *Wait that's Camille's last name, there is no way, but I mean it's hyphenated. It has to be.* I pick the phone up to call her, but realize it's too noisy and I probably shouldn't call from the air.

When I arrive at the house, there's a vase full of tulips on the porch steps. The note attached to them reads: *I can't wait to get to know you on a deeper level. See you soon.*

I let out a deep sigh and look up at the stars. *They should know not to send me flowers. I need to find out with a quickness and put a stop to it.*

After checking to see if there are any messages from Tori, which there aren't, I take a long shower. While in there, I think of a way to ask the only two people who would've sent the tulips if they're responsible, but without letting them know someone else may have sent the flowers.

Before sitting on the bed, I open the double doors to the balcony to let in some fresh air. While putting lotion on, I get the feeling that someone is watching me, so I quickly turn my head toward the doors.

I've been paranoid like crazy lately.

I don't see much. Just shadows through the now bare trees and what looks like a telescope in one of the windows of Mrs. Johnson's house.

I'm going to have to pay her a visit soon.

12

Camille follows me into my office and closes the door behind us. She isn't her perky self this morning. I know because she didn't flash her teeth at me.

Instead, she raises her eyebrows and says, "Tuesday mornings. Don't you just love Tuesdays?"

"Sure. Everybody loves Tuesdays, Cam. Have a seat, and tell me about your yesterday and this morning."

She tells me she didn't do much yesterday, just her assignment, and then she hung out with her little man, as she calls him. This morning, she woke up a little anxious, but that's about it.

"Do you want to talk about it?" I ask.

"No, I'm good."

"Okay then, Camille, let me ask you a question."

"Umm hmm."

"If you were gonna send me flowers, what kind would you send me?"

She smoothes the wrinkles out of her pants and pulls on the collar of her shirt. "Well, Ms. Morriston, I would not send you flowers."

I lean back in my chair. "Oh, really? Why not?"

"Do you really want an answer?"

I look at her in a demanding way.

"Because Ms. Greer may get them before you do."

While I'm surprised it took her this long to find out about Victoria, I'm still shocked she said it.

I clear my throat and go on the defensive. "I see. Victoria. Is she what has you in a somber mood this morning?"

She stares at me, shaking her head.

"All right, Camille. You get two minutes to ask me all the questions you need answers to about her. So you better make them good. But first, let me clear some things up. She left me and went back to Wisconsin, but no one in this office knows that, and I want to keep it that way. We were on the outs when I met you. I was trying to work it out with her at first, but it didn't work, so now I'm moving on with my life. Now, you may ask your questions."

"You know, I thought I had some, but I don't want to ask you anything about your past relationships. My dad always told me—only ask questions if you're prepared for the answers."

"Ah, speaking of your dad, I Googled your name last night."

She puts her head in her hands.

"Lift your head up. People might think I'm chewing you out if they walk by, and it's only day two."

"Why did you Google me? I mean, do you Google everyone? Is that your thing?"

"Well, for one, you're my intern. But, for your information, no. I saw your last name from the sky last night."

"How did you see my name from the sky? What does that mean?"

"It doesn't matter. What I've been trying to figure out is why you were a stripper."

"Oh, wait. You have me confused with that other Camille Jerkins-Borders girl. I'm not the one—"

"Camille, don't bullshit me," I interrupt. "You look just like that family."

"I know. I get that all the time, but it's not me. I mean, really. Would I be a stripper if my family owned the largest African American greeting card company in the world? Really think about it. Honestly, I think it would be kind of disgraceful. Shoot, if I were them, I would probably disown me, too. Their only daughter a stripper? How outrageous!"

"You sure do know a lot about them."

"I mean, duh! If enough people mistake you for someone, you would find out who they are, right?"

"So why were you acting all funny about me Googling you?"

"Because I think it's weird to randomly Google normal people. Makes me think you're paranoid."

I stare at her blankly because I can't tell if she's being serious or not. I know she's their daughter.

"I'm joking with you, Laila." She takes a pause. "I don't think you're paranoid."

"Well, I think it's you, Ms. Jerkins-Borders."

"It doesn't matter if it is. I'm here to intern for you, so that's what I'm going to do."

Her cockiness amuses and excites me. I want to do things to and with her that I said I would only do with Tori.

I don't know what has gotten into me lately; it's like I'm in sexual overdrive. I want to have sex all the time and everywhere. I need to make an appointment with my psychiatrist, Dr. Rivers. Maybe she can help me figure out how to get my life back on track.

"So, how did you hear about Tori?"

"Oh, it doesn't matter," she replies.

"You're not going to tell me no matter how hard I press you, huh?"

"Nope."

"Well, then—what other rumors have you heard?"

"Not anything worth mentioning. Just that you're a real hard ass."

"Well, if there's nothing else to share and you have no questions for me, I guess you can go get started on your work. By the way, we're having lunch today. I'll text you the details."

As she walks out of the office, she says, "Oh, yeah, there was something about a scandal with an ex-secretary of yours being infatuated with you, and they had to fire her and a bunch of other people."

What in the world is she talking about? I didn't hear anything about that.

"Wait. What exactly did you hear?"

"I just told you. That's all I remember."

"Well, if you remember anything else, let me know. And watch for that text message; follow the directions in it to a T."

After Camille leaves my office, I walk down to John's office to find out more information about this rumor. He gives me an earful about Tasha, and I'm convinced she's a little off. When I ask him why no one said anything to me before, he says they didn't want to alarm me.

I have to figure out how to get rid of her. I can't tell John she's my driver 'cause I don't want to get her into more trouble. I should be able to take care of it myself. Tomorrow's dinner will be interesting. I'm going to have to get Trey to go with me.

As John and I are walking back to my office, we see Mrs. Spady and Nadia coming down the hall with six Panera Bread employees behind them. John, with his ass-kissing self, almost took off running when he saw all that money coming down the hall. One time, he told me that when he sees really rich clients, he pictures them as dancing Sims Avatars with dollar signs over their heads. He's such a gold-digger.

Mrs. Spady stops in the middle of the office and announces that since she is so pleased with the work John and I have done, lunch is on her. The whole place erupts with gratitude.

Mrs. Spady points, walks toward me, and says, "Say thank you to Ms. Morriston."

Nadia chimes in after her, "And Mr. Twit for their great work."

Mrs. Spady asks John if he can manage the food set-up before the three of us go into my office. We have a short meeting, and I ask if either of them sent anything to my house yesterday. They both say no, and I believe they didn't. Nadia looks at me with an expression that lets me know she will ask me about it later.

When Mrs. Spady and Nadia leave, I call Trey to tell him about Tasha.

"Trey let me tell you about Tasha's crazy ass."

"See? Before you start, I told you something was wrong with that girl. You never listen."

"Get this. Apparently, she was rambling on and on in the bathroom one day about how she's in love with me. Turns out she was talking to someone who she didn't know was the client of a top associate here."

"Oh, my! Wait! Isn't she still driving you?"

"Yes. I'm not sure how she pulled that off. It's scary, though, *and* she has guiled me into going to dinner with her. Will you go with me to keep a lookout?"

"Girl, yes. You know I got your back. What are you doing for lunch today?"

"I'm having lunch with Camille."

"No, no, no, Laila. You need to stop. I told you to stop hangin' with that woman."

"We're just having lunch, Trey."

"And lunch is doing too much. You need to carry your ass to Wisconsin and get Tori back."

"She left me, remember?"

"I know that, but running around with someone else ain't gonna do any good."

"Look, Tori left me, not the other way around. I'm tired of chasing her. We can talk about that later, though, okay?"

"I'm just saying—you need to chill 'cause you actin' like you have lost your damn mind."

"I just want to see what else is out there. It's pretty much a wrap with Tori and I."

"Well, you haven't officially thrown in the towel yet, so you need to leave those other women alone, Laila."

"Bye, Trey!"

"Whatever. You know I'm right! Until you officially break up, keep your shit in check. Goodbye."

Camille follows my directions perfectly, and we end up having a great lunch date.

I'm practically single, so there's no reason I can't date, right? I just have to watch it at work with Camille.

13

After being irresponsible for the past five months, I go to the gynecologist to have a complete STD test and annual exam done. I want to make an appointment to see the dermatologist, but it would be just to see Christina. Tori and I have been coming to the same OB-GYN for the past four years, and most of the time, we go together. I was hoping, in the near future, we would start thinking about children, but that's not going to happen.

"Hello, Ms. Morriston. You're in early this year."

"I know, Dr. Gray. I figured I'd get my exam done sooner rather than later."

"I can understand that, given the circumstances."

Given the circumstances? What does he mean? I wonder if Tori knows and told him something.

"I have a question. By any chance, are you able to rush the results?" I ask him nervously.

"I think I can get that done for you. Relax for me, Ms. Morriston. I'm almost done."

"Okay. I would appreciate it if you could."

"Ms. Morriston, I need you to do me a favor. Can you tell Ms. Greer to come in and see me? She's missed her last few appointments, and it's important that I see her."

What's going on? Why has she been missing appointments? But, more importantly, why has she been making them? I wonder how many she's missed. I should ask, but he probably won't tell me.

"Okay, Doc. Is there anything I need to know about or that I can tell her to get her to come in? You know how she is."

He pulls the speculum out of me and pats me on the leg. "No, and don't start worrying. If you could tell her to call me or stop by the office that would be fine."

As soon as I step outside the doctor's office, I call Tori, and surprisingly, she picks the phone up on the first ring. I hear her laughing before she says hello. I haven't heard her laugh that hard in a while. You know the kind of laughter when someone tickles you so hard you want to pee. It puts a smile on my face.

"Hello, Tori!"

"Laila?" she says in a surprised voice.

"How have you been? It's good to talk to you, dear."

"I've been good. Umm, I've been trying to call you," she tries to say convincingly.

"Really? Something must be wrong with my phone, and the house phone, too, 'cause I haven't gotten your calls."

"Yeah, maybe. Wassup?"

"I was calling to check on you and talk about some stuff, but it doesn't seem like the right time."

"Yeah, we're in the middle of family games 'n stuff."

"Oh... Well, I won't keep you. But Dr. Gray told me to tell you he needs you to come by the office for something."

She takes an extremely long pause, and the background noise fades away.

"Hello? Tori? You still there?" I ask.

"Okay. Did he say anything else to you?"

"No."

Her voice becomes monotone, which lets me know she's hiding something.

She presses me for an answer. "Laila, did he say anything else to you?"

"No. He just said it's important that you come in. Tori, is there something you need to tell me? Did you catch something and not tell me?"

"No, it's nothing like that."

"Listen, if you did, you can tell me. I won't get that mad. Shit happens, and I know we haven't been in the best place lately."

Shoot, I might have just thrown myself under the bus.

"No, it's nothing like that, okay?"

"Well, what is it then? Why is it imperative that you come see him, Tori?"

"Look, my mother is calling me. I think it's my turn. Can I call you back?"

"I don't have a choice, do I? Look, when are you coming back? I miss you."

"I don't know. I'll text you."

"You'll what?"

"I love you. I have to go."

The phone goes silent in my ear.

She irritates me so much sometimes. The worst thing about Tori being away is that she can hang up on me all day, avoid my calls, and I can't do a damn thing about it.

Ugh. I absolutely hate not being in control. I should go back in there and see what info I can get from the nurse, but I know they won't violate any of those damn regulations they abide by. I really need to figure out a way to get Tori back here. She's one of the few people who know how to get underneath my skin. Love can be so bittersweet.

The buzz from my vibrating phone jolts me from my thoughts. It's a text message from Tasha reminding me of our date tonight. It totally slipped my mind.

* * *

While preparing for dinner, I try to figure out exactly what I'm going to say to Tasha. Since I already know she's off her rocker, I have to approach the situation with caution. Firing someone is not easy, but this is going to be a serious challenge. I need to find out what happened to Michael.

The doorbell rings, and I take my time answering it. The person rings it two more times before I finally open the door. When I do, I see Nadia's five-foot self-standing there. Her shoulder-length hair is pulled back into a single ponytail, so all of her facial features are illuminated by the moonlight. Her almond-shaped eyes are gleaming, and her eyebrows are perfectly arched. It's hard for me to believe she doesn't get them done. Her skin tone is a beautiful, deep milk chocolate, and her hazel eyes are perfectly juxtaposed against her even tone.

"Nadia, what are you doing here? You look amazing."

"I know I shouldn't have popped in on you like this, but I wanted to see you. It looks like you're getting ready to go out, though. I'm sorry. This was inappropriate. Please forgive me. I'm gonna go."

"No, no. It's okay. I'm getting ready for dinner, but come in."

"I'll only stay a few minutes. Please don't be upset. I don't know what I was thinking. I'll never pop up on you again."

"It's cool, but a call would've given me some time to prepare for your visit."

"You know what? I can go. Get ready for your dinner, okay?" She's about to turn around and head toward the door, but I stop her.

"No, stay. I can get ready and talk to you at the same time."

"What time do you need to leave?"

"In about an hour. I'm taking Tasha out to dinner tonight."

"Oh, that's nice."

"Not really. I have to fire her."

She laughs. "What? You're taking her to dinner to fire her?"

"I love your laugh, you know that? It's good to laugh. Anyway, we planned the dinner the other night, but since then, I found out I have to fire her."

"What happened?"

"Long story. Don't want to get into it. Come upstairs with me."

We go into my bedroom and sit on the bed for a minute to talk. I sense Nadia is nervous, so I open the balcony doors to let in some fresh air. When I do that, over at Mrs. Johnson's house, the light in the room directly across from my house goes out.

I walk back over to the bed and kiss Nadia on the neck. She tenses up when I brush my tongue across her ear. I place my nose against hers and tell her if she wants it, she has to make the first move, and then I make my way to the bathroom.

I'm letting my libido get the best of me, and I need to stop it before someone gets hurt. I'm in a messed up place emotionally and mentally, and I don't need to drag anyone further into my mess.

Unfortunately, Nadia never comes into the bathroom with me. When I'm putting in my second earring, she tells me my phone is vibrating. I run out to check it. It's Tasha cancelling on me.

"It's your lucky night, Nadia. Tasha just cancelled."

I send Trey a message telling him dinner is off and then I throw my phone on the bed.

"Really! I mean, sorry to hear that."

"To be honest, I didn't want to go anyway. Can you help me get this dress off? It was a pain putting it on."

"Sure."

I turn around and put my hands above my head while she unzips the dress. As I suspected she would, she feels me up, but only a little bit. I ask her if she's nervous.

"I'm afraid if... if I touch you too much... I might do something before I'm ready."

I turn around and pull her into me. "Don't rush into anything. I don't want you to feel like I'm pressuring you. It's going to be a special moment for you, so it should happen the way you want it to. And it doesn't have to be with me, okay?"

"Thank you. I want you, and I want to do it now, but..."

"But what? Don't get all shy on me. We're working on that, remember?"

"I have to ask you something that's important to me."

"Ask me anything," I say without hesitation.

"Umm, did you, and... well... do you and Tori get STD checks regularly?"

I take a deep breath. *Whew! I didn't know where that was going.*

"That's your question? Babe, let me tell you something. Don't ever be afraid to ask someone you want to be intimate with about his or her status. Just because someone is a lesbian or predominately sleeps with women does not mean anything. They're not immune to STDs, and just because they are faithful, that doesn't mean their partner is. Oh, and viruses and bacteria can live on some toys. So, always ask about that."

She has a look of relief on her face.

"But, to answer your question, we do get tested together every year just because. I personally had it done not too long ago. The results should be back in a couple of days."

"Really? That's good! I'm glad you... well, you both get tested regularly."

"How about we go to the Redbox, get a movie and a bottle of wine from somewhere, and just chill?"

She says, "As long as it's a comedy."

* * *

Nadia wakes me up with a kiss on the forehead at three in the morning. I try to convince her not to leave, but she insists and tells me to call her after I get off work. That probably means she wants to come back over, but I have plans with Camille. This is getting way out of hand; I let someone else stay in my house. And while it may not seem like Tori is the person I truly want, I miss her like crazy. She's never left me before. I mean, we have pulled stunts on each other, but this is serious.

Stop being naïve, Laila. Her actions say she's done with you.

14

Camille is excited when I see her, but I have too much on my mind to entertain her. Tasha woke me up early this morning screaming about how I've been letting her down lately, about how I need to get my life together, and that I need to leave Nadia and Camille alone. She was yelling about how I don't need to love them and they are no good for me. I hung up on her twice, but she kept calling me back, so I let her rant for about ten minutes before I told her I was going to call her back. She might be crazier than I thought. I don't even remember all of what she said, but she was telling me how I can't see what's right in front of me and I'm a selfish bitch. Her comments threw me off because I didn't know my relationships with Nadia and Camille were obvious.

She had one thing right, though—I am being selfish.

Camille notices my frustration and adjusts her demeanor by becoming calmer. She tells me that she should have her project completed by the end of next week. It would be better for me if she completes it sooner.

"Cam, let's make a bet. If you get it done by the end of this week, I will pay Jeremy's tuition for two months."

"And if I don't?"

"Well, you will just have to wait and see."

"A blind bet? I don't know if I like that, but if it's anything like what went on the other day, I'm down."

I smile at her. I was extremely horny the other day, so we had sex on our lunch break.

"If you take it blindly, you get to pick something else on top of his tuition."

Sticking out her hand, she says, "I'll have it done by Friday."

We shake on it, and she leaves my office. Fifteen minutes later, she pokes her head in the door.

"I need to cancel tonight. Sorry, but I have work to do."

I look at her and shake my head. "You're serious, huh?"

She winks. "I'm booked for the rest of the week."

I wave for her to come in. She stops short of my desk, and I tell her to come closer.

"But what am I going to do when I want you to fuck my brains out?"

She leans down on the desk like she's reading something and says, "Masturbate!"

"Smart ass, get out."

She winks at me, then walks backwards out of my office. Shortly after she leaves, John comes in with a project offer for me to review.

"Laila, do you want this one, or do you want me to give it to Malik? He doesn't have an intern to deal with."

"Is it a small job or a big one?"

"A decent–sized one."

"I'll take it. I haven't had anything that's taken me longer than four days to complete since the Spady job."

"Are you sure? I don't want you to be overwhelmed by this and your intern. You know how moody you get when you're in the zone, as you call it."

I laugh because he's right. "I don't get moody, John. Just focused."

"How is your intern? You know who she is, right?"

"She's doing well, and yes, I know who she is."

"Look, between you and me, the execs are talking about trying to hire her."

"Let me guess. Because of her name, right?"

"Exactly, but you know it's supposed to be kept under wraps."

"But what if she doesn't—"

"Look, you just make sure she does well and her presentation goes off without a glitch."

I look at him snidely and shake my head. *She may not even want to work here, and they're already planning her future here.*

"Laila, I'm serious. This is a big deal." John says.

"Why is it so important?"

"All I'm going to say is that we're trying to go international."

"Gotta love the business world."

"Oh, they found you another driver. Yours quit this morning. This one will double as a bodyguard."

"Is it really that serious?"

"It's just a precaution, Laila."

Damn, I wish I had been just a little bit nicer to Tasha.

* * *

Nadia and I have another fun night of drinking and movie watching. She tells me so much about herself, but I still think she's hiding something. Even if I'm right, I'm in no position to judge. Victoria, Camille, Nadia, and I all have our secrets.

* * *

It has been a long six days since I went to the doctor. I think Nadia was more ecstatic about my results arriving yesterday than I was. I let her open them because I was scared as shit. I tried to play it cool, but was frantic on the inside. I told her if all the tests were not negative, I was leaving for Wisconsin this morning. But the truth is, I probably would have just cried from embarrassment.

One of the reasons I like Nadia so much is that she's an easy-going person. I feel like I can sit down and talk to her about anything. She's such a sweet person, but very shy. We're working on her being more assertive. There's this easiness to her spirit that I can't explain, a certain calmness I want around me all the time. I wish I had met her under different circumstances and wasn't subjecting her to things I can't bring myself to tell her about. Every day, I want to confess my sins and apologize a thousand times, but I just can't.

I can't risk losing her. She's keeping me in a good place emotionally and I need that because I'm ready to call it quits.

Tori is running with bulls and milking cows in Wisconsin. Camille has me wondering if she's going to blow our cover at work. And Tasha? Tasha has me nervous all the time with all the love letters, flowers, and candy she constantly sends me.

I need to move away is what I need to do.

15

Camille only has two days to complete her project, or I win. I'm pretty sure I have this one in the bag because she's been panicked and a little distressed. Since Camille started interning, we've been having lunch together when I don't have other obligations. This week, she's forced me to actually eat with her, instead of having sex, which is fine with me because we have the most interesting conversations. I love being able to talk to someone who actually gets civil engineering—other than my co-workers. The downside to us not being physical is that we are connecting emotionally because I become too vulnerable.

"Laila, am I going to be presenting my presentation to the executives as soon as I'm done with it?"

"I don't know. I hope so. I want you to wait 'til the other interns present their work so you don't show anyone up."

"Yeah, you're right. They'll think I'm a suck-up. They already think I paid to intern with you."

"Did you?"

She wrinkles her brow at me.

"Chill, woman. I'm joking with you. Oh, I've decided what I want when I win."

"Okay. Well, do you want to tell me now so I have a head's up, or are you gonna make me wait?"

"Make you wait! It's only two days away."

"You want to have dinner at my place tomorrow?" Camille asks.

"What about Jeremy?"

"He's gone for the week. They're on spring break."

"Do you think I can get back to you on that?"

"That's fine. I'm gonna go now, if that's okay."

"Cam, lunch at one?" I say while winking.

* * *

I hear a commotion in the hallway, but by the time I decide to find out what it's about, it's too late. Tasha bursts through my office door, and my heart skips three beats. As she locks the doors, she tells me to sit down. I am stunned, frozen in place.

"Sit down, Laila," she repeats. "I don't want to hurt you. I just want to talk."

"How did you get past security?"

"Why haven't you retuned my calls? You said you would call me back, and we were supposed to reschedule dinner. What happened?"

"I know. I'm sorry. We can go—"

She cuts me off. "All you have to say is sorry? I love you, Laila, and you hardly even notice."

"Tasha."

"Shut up! Let me talk. I gave you so many hints. All those nights we spent working together, all those long rides together, you calling me whenever you needed something. You never got it, though, did you? You bitch! I know you care about me. I can see it in your eyes. Don't you love me? I love you. We're supposed to be together."

I see a crowd forming outside my office.

They should have a key. Hurry up and open the door.

"I do care about you, Tasha. You're a sweet girl."

Why can't they get in here? God, help me. Please help me.

141

I stand up.

"Sit your ass down." She places a gun on the desk.

"Tasha, this is not the way to get my attention."

"Well, I have it, don't I?"

"They're going to open that door."

"It'll take them a while. I changed the locks. Laila, I love you." She starts pacing back and forth faster.

"Tasha, why are you doing this?"

"Because you keep ignoring me. I just wanted to talk to you. Why didn't you call or email me back? Something! Oh... I know why. 'Cause you spendin' all your time with Camille sexing on lunch and sleeping with Nadia at night." She picks up the gun and slams it back on the desk.

Try to stay calm, Laila.

"ANSWER ME, DAMMIT!"

"If you don't want to hurt me, why do you have that?" I try to ask calmly.

My palms are sweating like crazy, and my whole body is shaking. I feel like I'm going to pee on myself.

"It's for them, not you, sweetie. I love you."

Help me, someone! Please, help me. God, please forgive me, for I have sinned...

Just then, the door flies open, and Camille rushes in and tackles Tasha from behind. A group of people enters after Camille to restrain Tasha until the cops arrive. I scream.

"How the fuck did this happen? How did she get in here? You told me she wouldn't be allowed in the building."

I start crying in front of everyone before I run out of the office and down the stairs to the parking garage. I hear Camille calling my name, but I ignore her. I can't stop running.

"Laila! Wait! Stop!"

Tears, mascara, and mucus are streaming down my face when I turn around. Camille runs up to me and hugs me tightly. I collapse in her arms, and we sink down to the pavement.

"It's okay. You're safe now."

I try to speak, but it's not understandable through the sobbing. Again, she tells me it's okay and to not say anything. Camille helps me up and walks me to my car. I'm glad she followed me because she brought my keys, purse, and cell phone out with her.

Camille and I sit in the car for a while until I pull it together. I see her in a totally different light now. She has secured a special place in my heart.

Who knows how far Tasha would have taken things. I'm forever indebted to Camille.

I lean over and kiss her on the forehead. "Camille, I'm so grateful."

I start crying again.

"Sweetie, stop crying. It's okay."

For a moment, I get beside myself and let the words "I love you" slip from my lips. She casually brushes it off, which I'm glad for because I don't know what I would have done if she had said it back to me. It was an accident.

I don't love her. At least I don't think I do. There's too much going on right now, too many emotions. I need Tori here to calm me down. I need her to hold me, to place my head on her chest so I can listen to her irregular heartbeat. That always helps me.

"Listen, why don't you go home and get some rest? I'm gonna go back to the office, okay?"

"Okay. Call me when you get off."

I drive around the city for hours trying to get into contact with Tori, but she doesn't answer. I'm afraid to go home right now, and I don't want to be alone tonight, so I call Nadia.

"Nadia, are you busy? I can call you later if you need me to."

"Slow down. What's wrong?"

Through sobs, I ask her, "Can I come see you?"

"Yes. What's wrong?"

"I just don't want to be alone right now. I'll tell you about it when I get there."

"Yes. I'm on my way home. You can come now. Do you want to stay on the phone?"

"No, I'm okay. I'll see you soon."

"Laila, call me back if you need to."

* * *

Nadia's knock on the car window causes me to almost have a heart attack.

"You scared me."

As glad as I am to see Nadia, my heart is yearning for Tori. She has been gone for more than two months now and still hasn't told me when she's coming back. This is the first time the thought that she might not come back has crossed my mind.

"Honey, what's wrong? What has you all upset?"

I get out of the car and hug her tightly.

"Oh, Nadia, the most awful thing happened to me at work, but I want to tell you about it later. Right now, I just want to pull myself together."

"Okay, baby. Let's go inside."

Inside Nadia's apartment, I finally feel safe.

"You rearranged your furniture," I say.

"Yeah, I do it twice a year. Do you want some wine or something?"

"No, water is fine. Thank you."

"Are you hungry? If not, I can make you a smoothie."

"No, I'm okay."

"Is there anything that will make you feel better?"

"A bath."

"Ahhh, let me go run the water. Do you want bubbles?"

I smile. "Bubbles are good."

144

Nadia smiles back at me. "There's that smile I've been looking for."

We go to the bathroom together, and I watch her prepare my bath. I walk up behind her and hug her. She turns around and kisses me gently. I can't remember the last time I took a bath. It's something I need to do more often.

Nadia leaves me to clear my mind, but it's so hard. I keep replaying the situation with Tasha over and over, trying to recall anything I may have done to lead her on. As for Tori, I've been so wrapped up in myself that she's probably left me permanently and I didn't even notice.

Nadia walks into the bathroom with a green smoothie and some fruit.

"You look stressed, Laila. You're supposed to be freeing your mind, remember?"

"I know. It's just hard to not think about it."

"Listen, I don't want you to get upset again. So, wait until tomorrow to tell me what happened. And drink this 'cause I know you probably haven't eaten."

"Thank you."

"Are you wrinkling up yet?"

"Not yet."

"Good. Drink your smoothie, and I'm gonna go find you something to wear."

"You're so good to me."

She smiles at me, and then leaves. *I wonder what she's thinking about.*

I finish my smoothie, bathe, and then make my way to her bedroom. As I'm walking to her room, I hear soft moans. I lean against the wall and listen to her for a minute. When she's climaxing, I go back to the bathroom quietly.

She would be so embarrassed if she knew I heard her.

I wait in the bathroom until she comes in. She brings me a pair of shorts and a camisole, and then she gets in the shower. I go to the bedroom and wait for her to finish.

145

By the time Nadia gets in bed, I'm fast asleep. A kiss on the forehead wakes me, but only for a moment.

She loves to kiss me on the forehead.

16

I need to get things in my life back in order. Yesterday scared the shit outta me, but in some weird way, I think I needed that to happen to gain some perspective. These two beautiful women are all caught up in my bullshit, and I need to fix it fast. I need to come up with a way to break things off with Nadia and Camille without causing a catastrophic event.

First, I need to break it off with Nadia before she finally gets the nerve to have sex with me. She desperately wants to, but gets nervous and can never go all the way. She's a level-headed woman, so I don't expect her to do more than get a tad bit emotional. The situation with Camille, however, is more delicate. I will wait until the internship is over to break it off with her. She could ruin my career if she wanted to.

Nadia rolls over and extends her arm toward where I was laying when we fell asleep.

"Laila?"

"I'm here."

Following the sound of my voice, she turns toward the window and sees me sitting underneath it with my legs crossed.

"Are you meditating?"

"No. I was sitting here watching you sleep. You're absolutely beautiful, you know that?"

She buries her head in the pillow. "Right now I'm not. I probably have crust in my eyes."

I move to the edge of the bed. "Let me see."

"Nooo, I don't want you to see it."

"Woman, I've seen you when you first wake up before."

"Yeah, from a nap, not eight hours of sleep."

I sit on the bed beside her and start tickling her. "Let me see."

When she does, I bend down and kiss her before she can protest.

"Laila, stop before I get embarrassed."

"Okay, okay. I'll leave you alone."

"What are your plans for the day?" she asks.

"I'm going to go home, and later I have a meeting with Camille."

"Do you want to stay here for another night?"

"I don't want to intrude on your space."

"It's fine. I enjoy having you here."

I say, "Is that right?"

She pulls the covers off and reveals her naked body.

"Damn, Nadia. Your breasts are beautiful."

"Well, come back later, and I'll cook for you topless."

I laugh at her. "I'll be back, but it'll be later than dinner time. Is that okay?"

She grunts a little bit. "Aww, I was looking forward to doing that. What time is it? I have to meet Mrs. Spady."

"Nine-thirty, I think."

"Shit, I have to go. Will you be okay?"

"Yes, and thanks again, Nadia, for everything."

She goes to take a shower, and I stretch out across the bed. Generally, I'm not a nosy person, and I don't like people going through my things, but I find something on her nightstand I can't ignore—a letter from the Pennsylvania court system.

148

After getting out of the shower, Nadia returns dressed. She's gone within thirty minutes. I need to take a lesson from her on how to get ready quickly.

Once she leaves, I wait about fifteen minutes before reading the letter. It's a petition to have child support payments increased.

Child support? She didn't tell me she had any children, and she sure as hell doesn't look like she's had any. I wonder why she doesn't have custody of the kid—or maybe kids. How come she's never mentioned it? Boy, oh boy, the skeletons people have. I need to end this relationship. How come Tori hasn't called me back yet?

On the way from Baltimore to Upper Marlboro, I think about how much I'm going to miss Nadia. We've cultivated a true friendship. It's going to be hard to break it off with her. Maybe we will remain friends.

Yes, I will shoot for that. Friends. We haven't had sex, so it should be okay.

Outside of Tori, she's the only other person who's made me feel like I can touch the sky. When I look into her eyes, I feel like I'm the only thing that matters in the world. I feel like everything that's wrong in the world can be righted. And maybe that's too much hope to place in someone, but I need to believe that people can be sincere.

At home, the answering machine is repeating: "You have two new messages." Both are from Tori. Apparently, she hasn't checked her messages because in one she says she's calling to tell me she loves me, and that her mother says hi. In the other, she says she lost her phone while riding her horse, Tax. She could have called my cell phone to tell me that.

I need to fix this. She has never been this upset with me, and I have never used anyone to take my mind off of her before. Hopefully, Dr. Rivers has an opening today because I really need some counseling.

I pack a bag for three days and clean up the house.

Recently, I've been realizing how much I miss all the things that annoy me about Tori. Some of the things I complained about incessantly just don't seem that important anymore.

Maybe I'm too stiff of a person. I need to learn how to loosen up.

* * *

At my therapy appointment, Dr. Rivers gives me some tips on how to end my relationships with Camille and Nadia, and also how to cope with the Tasha issue. She tells me how to work on getting past my own issues so I can forgive Tori. At this point, I'm being just as bad as she's been in the past.

All this lying and cheating is so messed up. I wonder if she knows about them and that's why she hasn't come back.

While driving to Camille's house, I call John and tell him to talk to the Bleakes, the CEOs of Expected Architecture, about getting me a new office. He understands I don't want my office to be as accessible as the one I have now.

Ugh, I should have taken what John was telling me about Tasha more seriously. No wonder Tori left. I've been so wrapped up in myself lately that I've been totally oblivious to what's been going on around me.

On the drive to Camille's, I try not to think about my problems, because all that's doing is depressing me, and I don't like being a Debbie downer.

Dinner at Camille's is always fun. Maybe it will ease my mind. It's sweet the effort Camille makes.

Since the beginning of our relationship, whenever we eat at her place, she has a raw food meal prepared. Camille and Jeremy are vegetarians, so she gets me being vegan, something Tori really doesn't understand outside of it being a healthy way to eat.

I buzz Camille's condo so she can let me in the building.

Over the intercom, she answers, "Hey, sweetie. I've been waiting on you. Stay in the lobby. I'm coming down."

She comes downstairs looking amazing. She has a fresh haircut, a pantsuit on that's not too masculine or feminine, and a pair of men's Louboutins.

"If you could come this way, Ms. Morriston," she says, while pointing down the hallway.

"Can I ask where we're going?"

She doesn't respond to my question. Instead, she leads me to the building's media room, where she's set up her presentation. I clap my hands in approval once we enter the room and I realize what's going on.

"Bravo, you got it done. I must say, I didn't think you would."

"Have a seat, please. The presentation will begin in two minutes." Camille dims the lights and lowers the projection screen.

"First, Ms. Morriston, I would like to thank you for providing me with this opportunity. It was a challenge recreating a project that I know you put your heart into. I hope my adaptations meet your approval and live up to not only your standards, but also those of the Environmental Protection Agency, and baseball fans as well. The first part of my presentation will be a PowerPoint on some of the new technology available that can be implemented in a stadium. Secondly... Well, you won't be disappointed."

It's amazing how fast technology advances. It's been five years since the new baseball stadium was built, and the stuff we used then already seems outdated. Along with the team at Expected, I tried to make it as eco-friendly as possible. I chose vegetation that captured the urban feel of the city but required the least amount of water to maintain it in a domed environment.

I will never admit it to her, or anyone for that matter, but the ideas she's come up with are fantastic. The second part of her presentation absolutely floors me. She's built a working model of the stadium. The miniature water recycling system actually works. It also has tiny solar tinted glass to show how the glass will help regulate the temperature in the building.

"I must say, you have outdone yourself, Ms. Jerkins-Borders. It was an amazing presentation. Now, how did you manage to put all this together in the eight weeks you've been interning?"

"Very little sleep and many forms of caffeine!"

"Did you do all of this yourself?"

"I actually did about seventy percent of it on my own. I even recorded it for the skeptics."

I clap my hands together one time and laugh. "Excellent! I'm glad you did, because people will question it."

"The slideshow only took about two days after I completed the research. The rest of the time was spent on the model."

"Wow, you're amazing."

"Thank you, Laila. That means a lot to me. Are you ready for dinner?"

"I am. What's on the menu, you?"

You just can't help yourself. Stop flirting! Stop flirting!

I ask another question before she responds to my first. "Umm… So, how much do I owe you for his tuition?"

"You don't have to give me money for that."

"No, a bet is a bet. How much, and what else is it that you want?"

"Are you sure? It's kind of expensive."

"How much?"

"For two months, his tuition is six thousand dollars."

Oh, that's some bullshit! That's what I get, though.

"You pay three thousand dollars a month? How much did you make as a stripper?"

She looks at me sideways.

"Okay, I'll get a cashier's check tomorrow. So, Camille, what else is it that you want?"

"Oh, trust me, you'll find out soon enough."

Dinner is great, and Camille fills me in on what happened at work after I left. Tasha was taken to jail, and everyone in the workplace was riled up, so they let everyone go home early. They were trying to figure out how she got in the building, and, furthermore, how the lock was changed on my office door. She tells me how no one is expecting me to come back to work until next week. She tries to get me to talk about my feelings, but I'm not in the mood. Tasha is locked up, so that eases my mind a little bit, but I know it will take me awhile to get over it fully.

I leave Camille's house at ten o'clock, an hour later than I would have liked, but she gets me so caught up. I call Nadia as soon as I get in the car. She picks up on the second ring.

"Hello."

"Good, you're still awake."

"Yes. I was finishing up this book."

"I'm on my way, if that's okay."

"Yes, it's fine."

"I'm sorry I'm coming so late. The presentation went longer than I thought it was going to be."

"It's okay. I may be asleep when you get here. Do you remember the alarm code?"

"Yes. See you soon."

After taking a shower, I climb in the bed with Nadia; she's asleep on her stomach, naked. I kiss her between the shoulder blades and snuggle up beside her. I'm almost asleep when Nadia asks if I'm sleeping.

"No, I'm awake."

"I'm ready," she exclaims.

"For what, honey?"

She turns onto her back. "You," she says, then puts my hand between her legs.

I softly ask, "Are you sure?"

Shit, Laila, you can't refuse her now. It would be weird.

Getting up on both elbows, she says, "Yes."

She climbs on top of me, and kisses me more intensely than she ever has. Her lips softly envelope mine and she slides the tip of her tongue in my mouth before quickly pulling it out. I slide my hands up and down her back as she kisses on my neck.

"Laila, you're so soft. I want to kiss you everywhere."

At first, all I want to do is get it over with, but I don't want her first experience to be a bad one. She's waited a long time to do this. I decide to go all in and give her the best sexual experience I can.

"This is your moment, Nadia. Do whatever you want."

"Are you sure, Laila?"

"Yes, don't be nervous."

She tells me, "I like your breasts," then she leans down and sucks on my right nipple while softly pinching the left one.

"You can do it harder."

She kisses, bites, and sucks on my breasts while I fondle hers. Then she works her way down the center of my torso before coming face-to-face with my vagina. She stops to look at it for a moment and then looks up at me.

"All of you is beautiful, huh?"

I laugh. I look down at her and see her eyeing me. I tell her to come up and kiss me. While we're kissing, I turn her over onto her back and take control of the situation. I slowly straddle her ass and then kiss the nape of her neck. She raises her hips and presses her ass into me. After kissing every part of her back, I tell her to get into a kneeling position.

Hugging her from behind, I whisper in her ear, "Just do what you're comfortable with."

She reaches backward, slides her hand between my legs, and finds my wetness. From behind, I grab one of her breasts and begin to rub on her clit. A couple of her fingers work their way inside of me. She lifts one of her legs and puts her foot flat on the bed. She pulls her fingers out of me and begins to moan while gyrating her hips against my pelvis. I tell her to lie back down, and I straddle her pelvis. I lean down and kiss her as she explores my body.

She says, "I love the way you feel on the inside."

After forty-five minutes of us fondling, grinding, and experimenting with different positions, she tells me that she wants to taste me. I reposition myself. She spreads my lips open and wraps her lips around my clit.

She says, "It's softer than I imagined."

I laugh to myself. Then she covers my whole vagina with her mouth and curls her tongue inside of me. I let out a soft moan.

She pushes it in and withdraws it a couple of times.

"It tastes better than I thought it would, too."

I laugh to myself and think, *Laila, what are you doing?*

17

I look out of my kitchen window and decide to make a stop before heading into the office. It's been three weeks since Nadia and I had sex for the first time. I've yet to break things off with her or Camille and Tori still hasn't come back from Wisconsin. Tori talks with me on a regular basis now, but feels we still need more time apart. If I had my shit together and wasn't so busy dating two other people, I could put some effort into coming to some kind of resolution with her, so we can end things amicably.

I knock on Mrs. Johnson's door months after I initially planned to.

"It's me, Mrs. Johnson. Laila Morriston, your neighbor."

She swings the door open, letting out the smell of eggs and bacon.

"Baby, you haven't come to visit me in ages. How long has it been?"

"About a year," I say.

"Come in, honey. You want some breakfast?"

"No, I'm going to grab something on the way to work."

"Are you sure? I have plenty. Eggs, toast, pancakes, bacon, sausages."

"No, I'm okay. Why'd you cook so much?"

"Well, normally, my granddaughter is here, but I haven't seen her in a couple of weeks. I'm hoping she'll come by. But, more so, it's out of habit."

"Where is she?"

"I don't know. She used to come by every other day, but then she just stopped."

"Why do you think that is?"

"Who knows? She's a little off, ya know. My family doesn't want to believe it, but I know, honey. Grandma always knows. Every time she comes over here, she stays locked up in that room with that dang telescope."

"Telescope," I say, like I don't know what she's talking about.

"Yeah. You wanna see it? The thing cost me two hundred dollars. I coulda got one cheaper at the flea market. Got me spendin' all my money all the time."

"Sure, I'll look at it."

Mrs. Johnson leads me upstairs to an office that sits off by itself, and there it is—the telescope I've been looking at from afar. I walk up to it and look through the lens. After repositioning it a couple of times, I find the exact angle that looks at the back of my house. I look straight through the trees into my master bedroom. You can see clearly into every room on the backside of the house. Once I see that, I tell Mrs. Johnson I have to go, and hastily make my way toward the front door.

"Well, Mrs. Johnson, I have to be getting to work now. I just wanted to see how you are doing."

I am filled with uneasiness.

"Okay, baby. Come back and see me again soon. You wanna take some food for the road? You look too thin, baby. Are you eating enough? You can—"

"No, I'm okay. Thanks, though."

I hug her goodbye and promise to come see her more often.

From the driveway, I yell, "Mrs. Johnson, what's your granddaughter's name?"

"Tasha. You know her?"

I take a deep breath and reply, "No, Mrs. Johnson. I'm afraid I don't." *I need to get my life together. How did I not realize that?*

At work, I have to put on my happy face because it's the last day of work for the interns. We always throw them a good luck party and bid them well on their future endeavors. At the luncheon, Camille receives an award for helping subdue Tasha, and everyone is released early. I ask Camille out for coffee and a walk through the park, I want to tell her about Mrs. Johnson being Tasha's grandmother. The main reason I ask her out is so I can break things off with her.

* * *

"It's a beautiful day to walk through the park, huh?" Camille says gleefully.

I hate what I'm about to do.

"It is! So, Camille, you made it. Now what? Two more months until graduation?"

"Yes, and I'm glad it's over!"

"So, what fields are you most interested in?"

"I don't know... maybe landscape."

"Oh, really? You truly are after my job, huh?"

"No, I wouldn't do that. I care about you too much."

Here we go. She's going to be emotional.

"Is that right?"

"Yeah, I do. I find you to be very interesting. As hard as you try to make yourself out to be tough, I know you really aren't. I can see past your cactus-like exterior."

I laugh out loud at her. "Cactus-like? What does that mean?"

"You're a survivor under extreme conditions, so you've built this hardcore exterior that no one wants to get close to because they're afraid. You're like a cactus, but I know how to navigate past all that prickliness."

Again, I laugh. "I see."

"That day... When you told me that you love me—"

Thankfully, her phone rings and interrupts her statement.

"Hold on. It's Jeremy's school." During the call, a panicked look comes over her face. "Look, Laila, I'm so sorry, but do you mind riding with me to pick up Jeremy? He fell and hit his head."

"Oh, my goodness! What happened?"

"I don't know. We gotta—"

"Yeah, yeah, let's go."

We head to Bethesda to pick up Jeremy, and Camille doesn't say a word the whole drive. I want to talk to her, but I let her focus on driving instead.

I love Bethesda. Maybe I'll consider moving out here if Tori and I don't make it.

We arrive at the school. Camille parks the car and takes a deep breath.

"Laila, listen to me. I know you're out and I am too, but can you please not be affectionate toward me in front of my son? I know that's a lot to ask, but it's a complicated situation that we can talk about later."

"Yeah, sure. I understand."

She returns about fifteen minutes later with Jeremy. It looks like they have a really good relationship. As soon as he gets in the car, Jeremy reaches over the backseat and greets me.

"Hello, Ms. Morriston. Do you mind if I call you Ms. M.?"

"Jeremy, son! I'm so sorry, Laila."

"Hello, young man. You can call me Ms. M. Can I call you Jeremy?"

"You can call me Lee. All my friends call me Lee, and it's one syllable. Easy to say."

"Lee it is, then."

Camille asks him if he has his seatbelt on, and then we head to I-495.

"Mommy, what are we going to do this weekend?"

"What would you like to do, honey?" Camille asks him in a tone I haven't heard from her before.

"Can we go to the zoo? I hear they have some new giraffes."

"If your head is feeling okay. How did you fall off the monkey bars anyway?" Camille asks.

In a whisper, he explains he was hanging upside down and his foot slipped. Camille gives him a short lecture on how he could have seriously injured himself if he'd landed worse than he did. He promises to be more careful, and she tells him she's not mad, just concerned. I smile at their conversation. Sometimes I wish I had kids already.

"Oh, Mommy, look! A truck just like yours. It's the same color and everything."

I look out of my window and see an Oxford white Mark LT. Sitting in the driver's seat of the truck is the damn secretary. I rise up out of my seat and stare in her direction. I want to start flailing my arms, but I can't. I have to contain myself. The woman never turns her head in our direction.

Please, let this be a big-ass coincidence.

The truck speedily pulls away, but not before I get a chance to read the license plate: AG LUV LM.

Alana Greer Loves Laila Morriston. What the fuck? I know she doesn't have that bitch driving her car! Come the fuck on. This shit is ludicrous.

I am so angry, I want to cry, but I can't. I won't. That would set off all kinds of alarms for Camille.

What am I going to do?

"Laila, do you want to have dinner with Jeremy and me?" Camille has to ask me the question twice before I respond.

"No, but thanks for the offer. I'm not feeling so well."

"Do you want me to stop by the store and get you something?"

"No, it's okay. Can you take me to my car? I'm gonna head home for the night."

"Are you sure?"

"Yes. You have a nice night with Lee."

* * *

When I arrive at home, I go on the warpath. I take all of Tori's stuff and put it in the basement, from her clothes to her toothbrush. I blow her phone up with message after message, demanding she get her ass back here.

"Tori let me tell you something. If you don't get your ass back here within two days, all hell is going to break loose on that Wisconsin farm."

As soon as I hang the phone up, Nadia calls.

"HELLO!"

"Laila, are you okay?"

"Yes."

"What are you doing? You sound out of breath."

"I'm rearranging furniture and putting all of Tori's shit in the basement. It's time to move it."

"Did something happen?" The softness of her voice calms me down a bit.

"It's just time, that's all."

"Do you want to talk about it?"

"Nope."

"Okay, listen... I called to tell you that I have to go out of town for a few days, but I'll be back Sunday if you want to get together."

"Where are you going, babe?"

"Pennsylvania. I have to go to court on Friday."

"Really? For what?" I ask.

"I'd like to talk to you about it face-to-face, if you don't mind."

"That's fine. Are you taking the dog with you?"

"No, he's going to Mrs. Spady's."

"That's cool. I'll see you when you get back then."

"Okay, I'll let you get back to rearranging."

Good, she got the hint that I want to get off the phone.

"Have a safe trip. Kisses."

My life is a total wreck, but tomorrow is a new day, and I'm going to fix it all. Hiatus, here I come. I need to go to India like that one lady in *Eat Pray Love*.

My phone rings, and I am hoping it's Tori, but it's Nadia again.

"Hey, honey."

"Laila, I have to ask you something. I wanted to do it in person, but I can't wait."

"Sure honey, wassup."

"I would like to elevate our relationship beyond dating... and be with you exclusively... be your girlfriend."

Shit, shit. Did she just ask me that? I can't say no. I mean, it is over with Tori. That was solidified today. There's no reason not to; we're practically already girlfriends, just without the title. I do care for her, and I plan on breaking it off with Camille.

"Laila, you there?"

"Yes."

"What do you think about that?"

"Yes, we can put a title on our relationship."

I can hear her smiling when she says, "Wow, okay. I have a girlfriend. Well, I'll let you get back to what you're doing."

I chuckle with joy. "Okay, baby. Call me whenever."

18

It's Thursday, and the sun's rays shining through the blinds wake me. I hate beautiful mornings when I'm in a terrible mood.

Ugh, what time is it? Ten-fifteen. Let me call out of work.

I swing my legs over the side of the bed, and my feet hit the wine bottle I finished off just before falling asleep. When I bend over to pick it up, everything starts spinning, and my stomach becomes queasy. Lying back down to catch my bearings doesn't help. I barely make it to the bathroom before the two bottles of wine I had last night erupt from my stomach. Most of it hits the floor, but I can't do anything about it right now. I grab the shower pillow, put it under my head, and then pass out on the cold floor. An hour later, I wake up again and throw up a second time after seeing the mess I made earlier.

Shit, I never called work.

I clean up the mess and take a shower before heading downstairs. When I get down there, I look at the piles of Tori's stuff. Suddenly, I remember why I made them, and I become angry all over again.

You know what, Laila. Go get your damn car. That's your shit! You paid for that out of your money. She let somebody else drive my car after telling me she parked it at work.

I make it to the dermatologist's office in two minutes.

While walking up the stairs, I give myself a pep talk.

Okay, try to stay calm. Just ask for the keys and get out of there with a quickness.

I walk into the office, and it seems like everything around me is moving in slow motion. There's one patient in the waiting area, and the secretary is filing her fake-ass nails. When she sees me standing there, she jumps to her feet and clears her throat.

"Hello, Ms. Morriston. Do you have an appointment today?"

"No! Where's my truck?"

"Would you like to go outside and talk?"

"No. Just give me my keys so I can leave."

"I don't have them on me, but can we please go outside?" she begs.

"No. I know you have them, so just give me my keys."

She comes from behind the reception area wall. "If we could please go outside, Ms. Morriston—"

"Just give me the keys, and I'll leave."

She puts her hand on my elbow.

I snatch it away, clinch my jaw, and through my teeth, I tell her, "Don't fucking touch me."

"I don't want to lose my job, so if we could please just go outside—"

"Fuck your goddamn secretarial job. Give me the keys so I can leave."

"I told you that I don't have your keys, and if you want them, you need to talk to Tori."

I see that the little old lady in the waiting area has become beet red in the face, so I agree to walk outside.

"Listen, Laila, how dare you come up to my job—"

"Bitch, don't talk to me. I came up here for one thing. Now, if you want it to turn into something else, don't come up off those keys."

"You threatening me? I may be a white girl, but I'll bust a bitch's ass."

Did she just get hood on me? What are you doing, Laila? Don't let her disrespect you. She knows you and Tori are together.

"Bitch, where the fuck is my truck?"

"I see what Tori be talking about... you never listening and shit."

"What? Speak up. Now you're an expert on my relationship?"

"No, but I know how to listen."

She is really trying me.

"You got about thirty seconds to come up off those keys!" I yell.

"I ain't comin' up off shit. You need to talk to Tori about all that. God, you don't listen. You're not listening now, and you wouldn't listen when she tried to tell you that she's pregn—" She stops mid-sentence and tries to walk away.

Was she about to say pregnant?

"Stand your ass still. What the fuck? She's what? What did you say?"

She continues to walk away.

Christina doesn't clarify. She just says, "Look, you need to talk to her about all of that. I have to go back to work."

I begin to cry. "Did you say she's pregnant?"

"Listen, I'm sorry, but you need to call her."

She leaves me standing in the parking lot stunned. After about two minutes, I get in my car and sit.

Pregnant! How did I miss that? All the signs were right there. OMG, I'm such an idiot. Have I been that wrapped up in myself lately? I'm so self-absorbed.

I call Tori, but her phone goes straight to voicemail, so I call Trey. He doesn't answer either. I leave him a message.

"Trey, I went to Christina's job and had it out with her. I'm coming over."

I leave the dermatologist's office and drive straight to Trey's. When I get there, I knock repeatedly and yell for him to open the door.

"Trey, hurry up! Trey!"

Matt opens up the door. "Laila, are you okay?"

"Is Trey home?" I look over his shoulder into the house. He steps to the side and tells me to come in.

Matt tells me Trey is in the shower. I barely say okay before I bolt up the stairs. I burst through the bathroom door just as Trey steps out of the shower.

In a high-pitched voice, he screams, "Oh, shit!" and quickly covers his genitals. I turn around and tell him I'm sorry.

He yells, "What's wrong with you, busting in here like that?"

Matt stands there shaking his head and laughing. When I presume Trey has fully covered himself, I turn back around.

"Trey, I've seen a penis before! But, look... I went to Christina's job."

"What is wrong with you, woman? Why would you do that?"

We leave the bathroom and go into the bedroom.

"Laila, you're losing your damn mind. Every day there's something new wit' you, I swear."

"I was angry... I mean, really upset. I guess when I saw her driving Victoria's truck, I snapped a little bit."

"That's understandable, but you're not twenty, Laila. You've got to get control of yourself."

Matt asks me, "So, what happened when you went to her job?"

"Well, it began inside. Then we moved it outside, and it got pretty bad. She told me she didn't have the key, but I didn't believe her. We were just going back and forth for a while, then she told me…"

I break down into tears and lie back on the bed.

Trey lies beside me. "Calm down, honey. What did she say?"

"I can't... I don't want to believe it."

"What is it, Laila?"

"That... that Tori is pregnant."

He quickly rises from the bed.

"Did I hear you correctly?"

I move my head in affirmation. He tells me to sit up.

"I can't."

"Laila, sit up, honey." When I rise up, he asks, "Do you think it's possible that she is... you know..."

"I don't know. I mean, some of the signs were there, but I don't know. Was I that disconnected?"

"Come on, Laila. You know you've had a lot going on lately."

"I know... but pregnant! I'm such an idiot."

"Listen, you need to go to Wisconsin. And you need to leave those other women alone. I keep telling you that."

"Trey, if she's pregnant, she cheated on me with a guy, and you want me to try to go work it out with her?"

"You need to go find out what the hell happened."

"No, I don't. It's apparent."

"Dammit, Laila. If she's straight now, then there's nothing you can do but move on. But you need to find out what happened."

My phone rings, interrupting our conversation.

"It's Tori."

"Well, answer it, dammit."

Tori asks me where I am. I tell her at Trey's.

"Well, can you come home?"

"You're in Maryland?"

"Yes, at the house."

"I'm on my way."

She hangs up without saying goodbye.

"Looks like I won't have to go to Wisconsin after all. She's at the house."

Matt says, "Maybe you should've gone to see Christina sooner."

"I know, right?"

"Well, you go ahead and go home," Trey tells me. "Call me if you need me, and don't come bustin' in on me like you the po-po again."

I start laughing really hard. "It was funny hearing you scream like a little girl."

"Get out and call me later."

"Bye. I love you."

When I get home, there are no pleasantries. Tori immediately starts going off on me.

"How dare you go up to Christina's job like that?"

Stay calm, Laila. You were wrong for that.

"I'm sorry, okay? I don't know what I was thinking."

"Yeah, that was real fucked up. Laila, sometimes you just don't think, do you?"

"I said I was sorry."

"You need to apologize to her."

"I won't."

"You're so rude sometimes, I swear. You need to apologize to that woman!"

"Why are you so concerned with her?"

"Because she's my friend."

Yeah right, just a friend.

The hostility drains from her voice after we go back and forth for ten minutes. "Look, Lai, you were dead wrong for going to her job, and you know it."

My phone rings and I answer it. It's Camille.

"Hey."

"Are you okay?" Camille asks. "I know you weren't feeling well yesterday."

Tori throws her hands up in the air and says, "Are you serious?"

"Yes, I'm in the middle of something now. Can I call you back?"

"Do you want to talk about it?"

I do and I wish I could with her, but unfortunately, I can't.

"No, I'll work it out."

"Okay. Call me later."

Tori shakes her head at me. "Why would you answer the phone in the middle of us talking do you see how inconsiderate you are?"

I quickly push the conversation with Camille to the background and refocus my energy on Tori. I don't answer her question. Instead, in hopes of easing some of the tension in the room, I calmly say I miss her and I'm glad she is back. It works.

In a melancholy voice, she says, "I missed you, too."

"Well, you sure don't seem like it."

We go into the living room and sit on the couch. As we are walking, I look at her. She has clearly gained weight, but she doesn't really look pregnant. Her stomach is slightly protruding, but it should be bigger, right?

I wonder how far along she is. She always gains weight when she goes home. Her hair is much longer, though, and so are her nails. Shit. Should I ask her about it? Clearly, she didn't want me to know. I wonder if the secretary told her I know. I should wait until she says something. No, I'm gonna ask. I need to know. I have a right to know. When did this happen? Wait...is she into guys now? Oh my goodness! She cheated on me with a guy! Now that one I didn't see coming.

Like Trey said, if she likes men now, there really is no hope for us. This just keeps getting worse and worse. I'm gonna ask. Wait! What if the secretary was lying? She really doesn't look pregnant. Her clothes are extra baggy, though. I'm gonna look into it more. Yeah, I'll do that before I say anything.

"Laila! Laila!"

"Hmm?"

"Why is my stuff all over the floor?"

"I...ugh. Ugh...honestly, I was putting it in the basement."

"The basement! What is wrong with you?"

"I just kinda flipped out yesterday."

"Over what?"

I go over and try to hug her. "We can talk about it later."

She pushes me away. "Laila, why did you move my stuff?"

"I was angry because that girl was driving your truck."

"WOW! Really, Laila, you could've called and asked me about it."

"I did call. You didn't—"

"Did it ever occur to you that I might not have had a signal all the time?"

"Oh."

"You are a real piece of work sometimes."

Wait a minute. I may have been wrong for going to that woman's job, but I'm not the only one at fault here.

She tries to walk away from me, but I grab her arm. "Wait one minute, Tori. Don't put all this shit on me like it's entirely my fault. You left me and now are acting like you're innocent. I've been trying to be cool, but you're making it real hard. Why did she have your car anyway?"

"You wouldn't believe me if I told you, so there's no need to get into it."

"See? That's what I'm talking about. How are you going to get mad at me for going to her job like you haven't done anything wrong? I need an explanation."

"You're stressing me out and I'm tired. So, let's talk about it later."

"Now you're tired? No, we're going to talk about this right now!"

She turns around with a horribly nasty look on her face, something I don't see too often. She's good at keeping her cool, so it always stuns me when she gets mad.

"Dammit, Laila, what did I say? I've been up for a long time, and I'm going to sleep."

Just like her to get tight-lipped when the conversation gets difficult.

"Can you just answer the question? Why was she driving your car?"

In a soft, matter-of-fact tone, she replies, "Because, Laila, her car was broken. I'm going to go to bed now."

I just look at her. The better part of me wants to flip out and curse her out, but I let her go upstairs. I go downstairs because arguing now would be pointless. My therapist tells me I need to stop being so argumentative.

While she's sleeping, my mind goes into overdrive.

I let her off way too easily because I feel bad about what I did. But, she had someone else driving her car. How did Christina get the keys? Something is wrong in this whole situation.

I decide I'm going to ask her if she is pregnant.

I walk into the bedroom and see Tori lying on her back. I try to stay angry, but can't. I miss seeing her in our bed. Gently, I sit down beside her and place my hand on her belly. It's bigger than I thought it was. She smiles and grabs my hand before her eyes pop open in shock.

"What are you doing?" she asks me.

"I came to check on you."

She rolls her eyes at me. "Well, you woke me up."

"I'm sorry, dang. Look, can you stop being mad at me for one minute? I'm really trying here."

"Why should I, Laila?"

"You're always angry, I'm always angry, and it has gotten us nowhere. Quite frankly, it's really starting to piss me off. You haven't been home in almost three months."

She rolls away from me.

"Oh, are you going to start ignoring me now?"

"I told you I'm tired. I was up late last night trying to pack. Then I had to wait stand-by to catch a flight to get back here. "

"I have a question."

She smacks the bed. "What is it, Laila?"

"Are you pregnant?"

When I ask her, I think she stops breathing for a couple of seconds.

"Yes," she quietly replies.

I take a deep breath and slink down, putting my head on my knees. "Why didn't you tell me?"

"Because I didn't know how to."

I get up, sit on the floor, and cross my legs.

"I tried to tell you."

I close my eyes and everything starts spinning. I open them and see her staring at me.

I ask her, "How far along are you?"

"About twenty-eight weeks."

"Twenty-eight weeks? That's like seven months." I stand up and start to walk out of the room.

"Where are you going?"

I ignore her and go downstairs, where I quickly grab my car keys and leave. She calls my phone ten times before I answer.

"Look, Tori, I just need some time!" I yell into the phone.

"It's not what you think. Come back so we can talk."

"I'm gonna call you back." I hang up before she can contest it.

I drive until I make it to Hollywood, Maryland. Along the way, I come up with a plan of what to do. Again, I decide to break it off with all three of them. That seems like the only feasible thing for me to do. I should've stuck to the plan the first time. First, I will break it off with Camille because she'll be the easiest to part from. I'll tell her that because of things happening at work, we can't keep our relationship going. Then Nadia, I feel like I may break her heart. I should have never slept with her. I let things go way too far with her.

I send Trey a text asking if I can stay at his house for a couple of days. I find the mall in Hollywood and buy a couple outfits and necessities so I don't have to go back home. By the time I make it to Trey and Matt's, they are asleep, so I quietly let myself in. I try to sleep, but my head is clouded with thought after thought of this mess I'm in.

I don't know why it didn't dawn on me before that Tori's pregnant. I really must be self-centered. Crap! Nadia asked me to be her girlfriend. This is not going to be good.

Erika Renee Land

19

I'm already awake when the first rays from the sun appear. I get up and go outside to watch the sunrise. It's the start of a new day, and I decide I must enact my plan as soon as possible. I make Trey and Matt breakfast and then leave for work. On the drive to the office, I call Krystal and tell her to set up a meeting with Camille for anywhere that Camille would like to have lunch. It would be inappropriate for me to call and set up a date with her just to break up. I need to keep this as formal as possible.

Goodness knows I hope this goes well.

At work, Krystal tells me that she cannot get in touch with Camille. Her phone is going straight to voicemail. I tell Krystal to keep trying because it's imperative that Camille and I meet today. Five minutes into me checking emails, Camille walks into my office.

"Camille, what are you doing here?"

"I needed to bring John the recording of me making the model."

"Oh! Did you get Krystal's message that I wanted to see you today?"

"No. I was just stopping by before I left the building."

"Oh, I see. Well, I have to talk to you about something important."

"Okay, I'm all ears."

174

I get up, close the blinds, and sit in the armchair next to her.

"Well, this is serious, isn't it?"

I instruct her to turn her chair toward mine so I can look her straight in the eye. She rubs her fingers across my cheeks.

"Laila, what's going on?"

"Camille, I'll be straightforward with you, because you deserve that and so much more—"

"Wait. Are you breaking up with me again?"

"Yes, and I'm sorry, but it would be for the best."

She drops her head and starts laughing. "Laila, are you serious? You break up with me every other week. You're just scared. That's all."

"No, I'm serious this time."

"You always say that, too. Whenever you start feeling too emotional, you break up with me. I'm used to it. I get it."

"No, Camille, I'm serious this time. I know in my heart we won't work."

"You say that now, but in a couple of days, you'll want to have sex. Then what? We'll be havin' this convo again."

"Camille, listen to me. I'm sorry I keep confusing you, but from this moment on, I won't anymore. We can't be together."

"Is it because they offered me a job here? I don't have to take it."

Noooo!

"Yes, love. That's exactly it. Things will be too complicated if we stay together. I'm sorry, I should not have—"

"Fuck. You're really serious this time, huh?"

"Yes."

She lets go of my hands, resets her chair to its original position, and leaves without saying anything else. I want to contest her walking out, but I know it's best I let her exit quietly. When Camille leaves my office, my heart begins to ache. I've always tried to detach my feelings from her, but the truth of the matter is a part of me loves her.

I think she really understands that it's over this time. I need her to understand that, it's for the best that we part, because nothing good will ever come from my relationship with her. What begins in chaos ends in chaos.

I send Trey a text letting him know that I broke it off with Camille. He replies, telling me to keep the lines of communication open with her so I'll know where her head is.

Since I no longer need to meet with Camille, I take Krystal out for an appreciation lunch. We visit a couple of building sites to make sure everything is on track with the projects, then return to work.

As I approach my designated parking space, I see Tori's truck parked in my space.

Remember to take the extra entrance pass from her.

I pull up behind her, and she jumps out of the truck. I tell Krystal to go ahead into the office and to make sure my schedule is clear for the rest of the day. I get a feeling this is not going to go well. Tori walks to the passenger side of the car and opens the door for Krystal. Once Krystal is on the elevator, she gets in.

"Is she the one who replaced Tasha?" she asks.

I roll my eyes at her, as she gets in the car.

"Yes, and I'm still upset because you weren't here for me when that happened."

"I'm sorry, Laila. Are you ever gonna tell me all of what happened?"

"Why are you here, Tori?"

"Because I'm tired of us fighting and running away from each other."

"I am, too. Do you think I like fighting with you?"

"Can we go for a drive?"

She looks like she has something pressing on her mind, so I comply with her request and slowly pull off.

"Have you eaten, Tori? Do you want to go get something?"

"No. Can you just drive around for a while, baby, and let me talk? This is going to be difficult for me to get out Laila."

I place my hand on her thigh and tell her, "Just be truthful with me, okay? I can't promise you anything, but I'm willing to listen."

Tori is silent until we get on I-395. Tears roll down her cheeks, which she quickly wipes away, and then blurts out, "Laila, I was raped."

I almost hit the brakes when I hear the word 'rape' leave her mouth. She tells me to keep driving and continues.

"I've been having a really tough time dealing with it, and I didn't know how to tell you. I've tried many times, but it just wouldn't come out. Actually, it has taken me a while to actually be able to say that out loud. I know you think I've been cheating on you, but I swear on Tax that I haven't."

"When did it happen?"

"The day...the day…"

The sound of her sobbing brings forth the memory of her crying in the shower. The night that spawned all of this was almost eight months ago.

The front door slammed, and Victoria ran upstairs before I could say, "Hey, babe." The shower started in the master bedroom, and an hour later, it was still running. I went upstairs and found her sitting on the shower floor shivering from the cold water. She was staring blankly at the blue-and-white-tiled wall.

"Baby, you okay?"

No response. I softly nudged her. "Baby, you okay?"

She responded, "Huh? Yeah, I'm fine."

"Tori, are you sure?"

"Yes."

"Baby, look at me."

She looked up, and I noticed that one of her eyes was swollen shut.

"Oh my goodness, baby! What have you been doing? Your eye is—"

"Huh? Oh, I was at the gym and had a bad sparring match."

"Sparring match? Since when do you spar?"

"Since not too long ago, and why all the damn questions? Just leave me alone. I'll be out soon."

I reached out to touch her. "Baby, why are you yelling at me?"

She gently pushed my hand away and asked me to leave her alone for a minute. I left and waited for her to come out. Twenty minutes later, she emerged.

"Baby that was the longest shower you have taken in the eight years I've known you."

"I know. Just had some stuff on my mind, that's all. I'm okay. Sorry for snapping on you. Would you mind getting me some ice?"

"Your eye looks terrible, what happened?"

"I was hit really hard."

We kissed and let it go. When we went to bed, she asked me to hold her until she fell asleep.

That night was eight months ago. Now here I am, flabbergasted, wondering how I missed it. I start to cry.

"You don't have to tell me, Tori. I know when."

"I'm sorry, Laila."

"No, stop. Don't apologize. I need to apologize."

"I should've said something, but I didn't know how to, and all I did was cause a bunch of problems."

"Let's go home, honey. We can get your truck tomorrow."

I'm absolutely floored by what Laila has told me, and I don't know what else to do but go home.

"I should have had this conversation with you a long time ago, Laila."

"Don't apologize, please. I'm the one who's sorry."

I want to ask her a million questions, but I don't think it's appropriate.

"I didn't know how to tell you. I just..." she starts shaking her head, and goes silent.

"Calm down. You don't have to explain yourself. I'm so sorry, Tori. I should have realized something happened to you."

I begin to cry silently; this guilt I have is overwhelming.

I should have listened to Trey. He kept telling me something was wrong with this situation. I have fucked up royally.

"Have you made an appointment to go see Dr. Gray yet?"

"No. I'll make one for next week."

Before Tori and I go into the house, I hug her for what seems like an eternity on the steps, while repeatedly telling her I'm sorry.

20

Inside the house, Tori and I begin our long road to recovery. She opens up to me and shatters all of the misconceptions I've had for the past few months. We go into the living room and lay on our oversized couch. I lay down first with my back against the arm of the couch; she then positions herself in front of me. While we're getting comfortable, I think of how much I've missed her. I stroke her hair and tell her again how sorry I am.

A small pool of tears forms on my inner arm from her crying, and she says, "It's not all your fault."

"I should have realized. All the signs were there," I say softly.

"I tried to hide it, Laila. Let me tell you what happened."

"You don't have to."

"No, I do. It's part of my therapy."

"Therapy? Oh, love," I say.

Tori tells me that she was running her usual route through the woods, when some guy came out of nowhere and attacked her. She tried to fight him off, but it didn't work. She stumbled to the parking lot afterward, and some people called the cops. She didn't think I would be able to handle it, so she didn't have South Mary Hospital call me. A couple of weeks later, she started going to group therapy meetings on Tuesdays and Thursdays, where she ran into

Christina. She says she was afraid, angry, and ashamed, and she should have been more careful. When she and I started fighting constantly, she couldn't take it and decided to visit her family in Wisconsin.

Tori tells me that Christina's car was broken, so she mailed her the keys to the truck. I'm not sure about that part, but I've been doing so much shady shit myself that I don't say anything about it.

Hours have passed by the time Tori stops speaking. We order some Chinese food, and I convince her to let me go pick it up by myself. When I'm in the car, I call Nadia, but she doesn't answer. I need to tell her we need to rethink our relationship. I've been so wrong about everything. My mind drifts to Camille, and I wonder how she's doing. I never meant to hurt her, but it was inevitable due to all of my untruthfulness. Her phone goes straight to voicemail too. I don't call her anymore.

At the Chinese food restaurant, I see Dr. Gray and tell him that Tori is back in town. He tells me if I can convince her to come by; he will open the office specifically for her tomorrow. I ask him if he's sure, because tomorrow is Saturday. He tells me it's not a problem and that he really needs to talk to her. I ask him if something is wrong, but he won't tell me anything. Only that it would be better if he saw her sooner than later. Dr. Gray's insistence on seeing Tori is making me wonder what's wrong.

When I get home, I have to wake Tori up so she can eat. I try to eat, but it's difficult because there are tons of things on my mind. She notices that I am playing with my food and asks me what's wrong. I want to put everything out there and tell her all I've done, but I can't. I'm afraid to tell her because of her fragile emotional state. So, to avoid upsetting her, I opt to tell her my thoughts about the baby.

"Tori, I want you to know that I am with you one-hundred percent on whatever decision you make about the baby."

"What do you mean?"

"Like if you decide to keep it or give it up for adoption. Have you thought about that at all?"

She shakes her head no. "I try not to think about it, like it doesn't exist."

I reach across the table and grab her hand. "Well, whatever you decide, I'm here for you. Do whatever you think will be best."

"I don't know. Adoption would be the only option, and it doesn't seem right to give your kid away if you're able to take care of it."

"I know. There's just so much to consider."

She stops looking directly at me and sits silently for a while. So, I move on with the conversation.

"I saw Dr. Gray while I was out getting the food."

"Really?"

"Yes. He wants you to come into the office tomorrow."

"On Saturday?"

"It's important, so I think we should go."

"I'm scared, Laila."

I hug her. "I'm here for you. You don't have to do this alone."

"Maybe I can wait until next week."

"Tori, you can't put it off. You've already gone long enough without seeing him."

She takes a deep breath. "I know. I'll go tomorrow, okay?"

"Okay. I'll call and let him know we'll be there."

She says, "I don't feel well. I'm gonna go to bed."

I kiss the top of her head. "Okay. Let me know if you need anything."

Watching her walk upstairs, I begin to think about the baby. I want her to keep it, but I know it will be unfair for me to ask that of her.

Tori looks so depressed. I'm going to see if she wants to visit my therapist with me.

While I'm on the phone with Dr. Gray, Camille beeps in, but I don't answer. Once I finish talking with him, I go upstairs to talk to Tori.

"Tori, I set the appointment. It's at ten."

She mumbles okay through the pillow.

"I'm going to Wal-Mart. Do you need anything?"

"No. Just be careful, okay?"

"I will. I love you more than anything, you know that right?"

She lifts her head and looks at me intensely for a moment. "I love you, too. Are you alright?"

"Yes. I'll be back soon."

On the drive to Wal-Mart, I call Camille. She doesn't answer, so I try Nadia.

"Hey, baby."

"Hey, Nadia. How are you?"

"I'm okay, a little stressed."

"How was court?"

"Ugh, draining."

My phone beeps.

"Shoot! Nadia, do you mind if I call you back? I have to take this call."

"No, that's fine. Call me back, though."

I take a deep breath and try to perk up. "Hey, Camille!"

"Laila."

"How are you doing?"

"I'm fine. Hurt, but whatever."

"Camille, I didn't mean to hurt you. It's just—"

"Unfair how you keep playing with my emotions!"

"I'm sorry, my life is just so complicated. I'm—"

"What, Laila, afraid? I've heard that before."

"Camille, listen—"

"No, I've got to go. Jeremy and I are about to miss our flight. Oh, but I do want to tell you that I accepted the job Expected Architecture offered me."

Breathe, Laila. Breathe. I'm in a world of trouble. Shit, I knew better.

I suck it up and say, "Well, congratulations are in order."

"Yeah, I accepted it about four hours ago. Anyway, I have to go. Have a good weekend. Bye."

"Camille."

She hangs up the phone without saying anything.

While walking around Wal-Mart, I get a massive headache. I go toward the medicine aisle and run into Christina.

There are way too many coincidences in my life. This day cannot get any worse.

She stands still and looks at me with a hateful look on her face.

"Look, Christina, before you say anything, I'm sorry. It was wrong of me to come to your job and act that way."

"Yeah, it was. You almost got me fired."

"I don't want there to be any tension between us, okay?"

"Yeah, that would be best, considering the circumstances. How's Tori?"

I get upset when she says Tori's name, but I don't react outwardly.

"She's fine, but I've got to get going, okay?"

"Alright. Tell her I said hi."

I pause for a moment and give her half a smile, before pushing the cart past her. I can feel her watching me as I walk away, but I don't look back. I find some medicine and pay for it then go back to shopping. I want to call Nadia and break it off with her, but she deserves more than that.

After walking around aimlessly for thirty minutes, I make my way to the baby section of the store.

I'm going to have to get Tori to see the reality of the situation. We have a baby on the way, and if she wants to keep it, we need to prepare.

Excitement overwhelms me as I look at all the things I want to buy. I wonder if it's going to be a boy or a girl.

Oh, I hope Tori wants to keep it.

I will have to remember to stay neutral and not try to convince her of what I want. We're going to have to definitely go to therapy. There's no way things will ever go back to the way they were, but we could use help on how to move forward.

When Tori calls and asks me to bring her some strawberries, I bring my trip to an end and head home. Tori is asleep again when I arrive, so I put the groceries away and get into the bed with her. I try to sleep, but I can't. I find myself glancing at the clock about every thirty minutes.

21

Tori and I arrive at Dr. Gray's office at exactly ten o'clock, even though she tried to delay coming as much as possible. When we walk through the door, we see Dr. Gray sitting there reading a magazine.

"Good morning. I'm glad you ladies showed up. I was worried."

I say, "I'm glad we made it, too."

He looks at Tori's belly, and she folds her arms across it.

"Why don't we get started? Tori, do you want Laila to accompany us?"

I stare at her, waiting for her answer.

She clears her throat. "Yes, it's fine."

In the exam room, Tori starts to cry while changing her clothes.

"It's okay, honey," I tell her. "I'm here with you. We will get through this together."

She repeatedly whispers, "I'm sorry," while I try to calm her. She sits on the exam table and puts her head in her hands.

"Try to calm down, honey. I know you're scared."

Then she blurts out, "Tori, I tried to kill the baby."

"What?"

"Remember the day I was really sick? I took an abortion pill—"

Dr. Gray knocks on the door, and Tori wipes the tears from her face before lying down. My face is frozen in shock.

"Are you two alright?"

Tori answers, "Yes," and I shake my head.

As Dr. Gray begins examining Tori, she starts to tremble, so he tries to reassure her it will be okay. He asks if she would rather Jessica, his physician assistant, perform the exam and then he could talk to us afterward. She declines and tells him to proceed. He looks at her belly and tells her to try and relax while he examines her cervix. Then he starts to give us bad news.

"Tori, I have to be frank with you. From looking at the size of your belly and with you being seven months pregnant, I think the baby may be in distress. When you came to see me all those months ago, the results showed that while the abortion pill you took did not kill the fetus, it did have some adverse effects."

I grab my stomach and listen while he continues.

"The fetus is developing, but it is smaller than it should be and some physical birth defects are present. Would you like me to show you on the ultrasound?"

I say yes; Tori says no. I go over to her and rub her head.

"Honey, we need to know."

She looks at me for a moment before finally saying okay.

Dr. Gray pushes the ultrasound monitor over to us and explains what we will see. Also, he asks if we want to know the sex of the baby. We tell him yes. The baby is below the average weight for this stage of the pregnancy, but physically where it should be. One of the baby's hands is deformed, and he informs us there could be severe brain damage, but there is no way to tell that right now.

Tori starts breathing rapidly, and we tell her to calm down. Dr. Gray tries to be reassuring and tells Tori not to come down on herself. I can't begin to imagine the things going through her head.

Once we get her to relax, he tells us that after we look at the baby's sex, we will be finished. He tries to perk up the conversation by asking what we would prefer. To me, it doesn't matter. Tori says a boy. He puts the ultrasound wand back inside her and finds the baby's genitals.

I ask, "Is that a…"

"Yes…it's a boy!"

I look down at Tori's face. She smiles a little and then puts her forearm over her eyes.

"Okay, ladies, that's it. I'm going to go to my office and wait for you there."

After he leaves, I tell Tori that she did great and that I'm proud of her. Once inside Dr. Gray's office, I ask him every question I can think of, but Victoria is completely silent. Before we leave, he asks us if we have given any thought to keeping the baby or not. I tell him I'm behind Tori in whatever decision she makes.

Breaking her silence, she says, "I want to keep him. I couldn't bring myself to give him away, especially since I…"

I grab her hand and squeeze it. She stops her statement, but we know what she was going to say. On the inside, I am doing flips, but I don't show my excitement because I'm unsure how she will interpret it, given the circumstances. Dr. Gray tells us we will have to come in weekly for check-ups and sends us home with about twenty pamphlets.

I look at my phone and see Trey has called me five times. I text him that I will be over in a couple of hours. Tori and I stop at Waffle House for breakfast. There are so many things I want to ask her, but I try to keep the conversation light and fluffy because I don't want her to cry. She hates being emotional in public. I ask her if she wants to go to Trey's with me, she declines.

"Do you want me to stay with you instead of leaving?" I ask. "You've been gone awhile, and I know we have a lot to talk about."

"No, I'm okay. I have to get an oil change anyway. I just want to think and digest all of this."

"Are you sure?"

She forces a smile. "Yes. Go have fun with your friend. Tell him I said hi."

* * *

When I get to Trey's house, Matt's car is gone and I'm glad, because there is so much I have to tell Trey. As soon as I remove my finger off the doorbell, he swings the door open and pulls me inside.

"Girl, you alright? Where you been? I was scared one of your women went loco on you."

I laugh at him. "Relax. I'm okay. Tori came to my job, and it was a long night. I have so much to tell you."

"Ooh, do tell, but first, I have to give you something."

He goes into the kitchen and comes back with a wrapped box.

"Trey, what's this for? It's not my birthday, is it?"

"I just felt like buying it for you when I saw it. Open it."

I tear away the wrapping and open the box to find a Coach purse with a matching clutch.

"Ahh, Trey, thank you. This is gorgeous."

"Girl, I know. I just had to get it for you, but you know it was on sale. Do you like it a lot or a little?"

"A lot...a whole lot."

"Good. Now tell me the latest news."

"Well, I broke up with Camille. That went okay. She cried, but left without incident. I've talked to her only once since, and she told me that she took a position at Expected."

"Hold it! Pump the brakes! She did what? Laila, that's not good, honey."

"I know, but I'm gonna have to deal with that later, because Tori told me that she was raped."

He stands up and covers his mouth. "Oh my! Oh no! Is she doing okay?"

"Not really. On the surface, she tries to be, but she is shattered. I can see it in her eyes. It's like that glimmer I used to see is gone now."

"Laila that explains a lot."

I plop backward on the couch. "I know, Trey. What am I going to do? I missed everything. The signs were right there. I'm such a fool." Tears start rolling down my cheeks.

"You need to fix things quickly, that's all. We'll figure it out, though."

"Treeeyyy."

"Yeah, I know, girl."

"Umm, Nadia asked me to be her girlfriend, and I said yes. Now, I have to break up with her, too."

He slaps my leg.

"Dammit, woman! Why did you do that? You know she's not going to take it well."

"I know...I know. So, I have to do it as gently as possible. She's such a sweet person."

"You know she ain't gonna get over it easy 'cause you were her first."

"I know, Trey, I know." I sit up and look at him. "Tell me what to do."

"You're on your own with this one. You're not gonna tear my head off later!"

"Trey, how did all of this happen?"

"Umm, let's see. You thought Tori was cheating on you, so you went out on the town and met Camille. Then you stalked the lady at the harbor."

"I did not stalk her."

"That's neither here nor there. What you did do was get these two women caught up in all of your BS unnecessarily."

"I know, but I'm gonna fix it. It's just hard because a piece of me loves them all."

"Grrrr! Laila, what are you talkin' about?"

"I feel like each of them fulfills a part of me that the others can't."

Trey huffs, "I am not even going to get you to explain that one! Just let Camille and Nadia go. Then you and Tori come to California with me and Matt and get married."

He lifts his left hand and shows me an engagement ring.

"WHAT? Married!" I exhibit more joy than I actually feel. I am happy for Trey, but I've got too many things going on in my life to feel overjoyed.

He starts screaming. "Ahh...yeeessss! Laila, I'm getting married!" He lays back and starts kicking his feet into the air.

"When did this happen? How did it happen?"

"Yesterday! It was so romantic, too. Ahh...I love him so much. We had dinner in Baltimore and then went on a helicopter ride over the city. There was a big group of people in the park by the harbor. Do you know which one I'm talking about?"

I pat his leg. "Yes. Yes, go on."

"Okay, so there was a big group of people, and as we were flying over them, they pulled out white cards that spelled out Will You Marry Me? Then he pulled out this ring. Girl, I burst into tears and screamed yes. Then fireworks went off that spelled out YES to the crowd. Then the crowd went crazy and popped like fifty bottles of champagne. "

"Oh my goodness, Trey! I'm so happy for you!"

"Laila, it was so beautiful."

I start clapping, "Ohh, we get to plan a wedding."

He starts smiling from ear to ear. "Unfortunately, no."

"Uhh, why not?"

"'Cause me and him got something better planned."

"What could be better than wedding planning?"

"Get this. We're going to ride a Greyhound bus from here to California, where we'll have a simple wedding. Forget all the glitz and glamour."

"Why a Greyhound?"

"We figure if we can make it across the country on a Greyhound without fighting too much, then all doubt will be eliminated regarding if we should get married or not."

I start hugging him again. "Wonderful, Trey. This is so amazing. I'm so happy for you. Have you set a date?"

"No. We're not going to rush it."

"Wow, this is wonderful. I can't wait to tell...Tori."

"What's wrong, honey? Why did your mood change?"

"Let's talk about it later. OMG! You're getting married! Wow."

"I know. I'm sorry we got sidetracked. Back to your story now."

"No, no. I'll tell you later. I have to go anyway. I told Tori that I wouldn't be gone long."

"Okay, girl. Tomorrow after you break up with Nadia, come by here before you go home."

I look at him with a long face. "Okay. I'll call you when I'm on my way to do it."

"Tell Tori I said hi. Kisses and drive safe!"

I wave goodbye as I am getting into my car.

* * *

When I get home, Tori is gone. I am extremely tired. Not sleeping the past two nights has caught up with me. While trying to nap, I get a text from Camille letting me know that she's not mad at me. I respond and then delete all of the messages and phone calls in my phone, lastly deleting Camille and Nadia's numbers. Tears are rolling down the side of my face onto the pillow. Finally, I pull the battery out of my phone and slide it into the space between the headboard and the mattress, just in case any messages come through while I'm asleep. I can't let anything happen that would derail Tori and I from our path of reconciliation.

22

Tori awakens me by rubbing her hand across my head.

"Hey, sweetie. What time is it?"

"Six-thirty."

"Oh. I wasn't asleep that long."

"Six-thirty in the morning, April third."

"Sunday?"

"Yes."

"Why didn't you wake me?"

"I tried, but you didn't budge. So, I left you alone."

I get up and go to the bathroom because my bladder is beyond full. As I enter the bathroom, I hear Tori tell me that she thinks I'm sexy. I smile to myself. I missed her compliments; she has always made me feel like the most beautiful woman in the world.

After I clean the twelve hours of sleep off my face, I go back into the bedroom and snuggle up next to Tori. I rub her tummy and ask her if she's ready for all that's about to happen.

Her response is, "I don't have any other choice."

"I want to know how you're feeling."

She kisses the top of my head. "I'm scared as sh...oh wait, we have to stop cursing. I'm scared out of my mind. So much has crossed it these past two days."

"Like what?"

"Like...will we be good mothers? What will he look like, and what should we name him?"

I tell her. "When he is here, we'll take it day by day, that's really all we can do."

"Laila, I hurt him, and I..."

"Shhh, shhh. Stop. Don't think about that. Calm down."

She starts breathing heavily, so I change the subject.

"Hey, Tori, guess what?"

"What?"

"Trey and Matt are getting married."

Through sniffles, she says, "Really?"

"Yeah."

"Wow! That's awesome."

"Oh, before I forget, I have a meeting later for a couple of hours."

I should be honest.

"When?"

"At about noon."

"Okay. Can we go to the health food store before you leave?"

"Sure, come on. Let's go take a shower."

In the shower, I am able to see exactly how much Tori's body has changed. She is so beautiful. She catches me staring, pulls me to her, and embraces me.

"I love you, Tori."

"I love you, too, Laila."

She lifts my head off her shoulder and places her lips on mine. We kiss under the falling water, and the familiarity between us sets in.

It's ten o'clock by the time Tori and I finish getting dressed and leave the house. We drive different cars to the health food store because of my meeting. When we get there, we have an amazing time shopping together. Tori is not normally into PDA, but she is being affectionate with me in the store. Our relationship has taken a turn for the better.

Time flies by, and it's eleven-fifty before I know it. Tori actually alerts me to the time. I pull my phone out and look at it. I have three text messages from Nadia. She is letting me know her flight arrived late so she's about twenty-five minutes behind schedule. I take a deep breath. Tori asks me what is wrong, but I can't tell her. So, I lie and say nothing. I spend five more minutes in the store with Tori, then I make my way to DuPont Circle where Nadia's favorite waitress works.

When I enter the café, I'm pleased to see Shay is working today. I ask to be seated in the section she is covering. When she comes over to greet me, I have a quick conversation with her before Nadia arrives.

I hand Shay a fifty-dollar bill and then tell her, "Listen, my friend is coming to meet me, but I can't stay long. After I leave, she may be very upset, so I want you to extend every courtesy possible to her. Oh, and by the way, she thinks you're beautiful."

She looks at me with a questioning look.

"Listen...please do this for me. Here's another hundred. Just make sure she's okay before she leaves. Okay?"

She says okay, then points behind me. "Is that your friend?"

"Yes. Please do this, and don't tell her I paid you. She's a really nice person."

Nadia comes over to the table and kisses me on my cheek before taking her seat.

"You look amazing, Nadia. I love the haircut."

"I've missed you, honey. What have you been up to?"

"I've been doin' a lot of thinking these past couple of days," I say.

She tilts her head; she always does this when she's worried. I reach across the table and motion for her to give me her hand. As soon as our flesh touches, I begin to cry.

"Laila, what's wrong?"

All I can say to her is that I'm sorry. I say it over and over again.

"What are you sorry about? What's wrong?" she asks.

"I have to...we have to..."

A waiter delivering our drinks interrupts me.

"Laila, what's wrong? What do you always say? Just come out with it."

"I'm sorry, Nadia. I love you, but we have to break up."

She lets out a hard sigh. "Laila, baby, you love me, but we have to break up? I don't understand."

"A lot has happened, and so, I just need to try to get myself together before I can be in a relationship."

"Well, what's going on? Maybe I can help you."

"No, you can't. I'm sorry, Nadia."

"So what? Are you scared because you're not over Tori? Is that it?"

I want to tell her the truth, but for some reason, I can't bring myself to do it. I'm being a coward.

"I don't have an explanation for you, honey."

"Don't you think I deserve one? Dammit, Laila! We've been seeing each other for months, and as soon as I ask you to commit to me, now we have a problem."

"Nadia, I'm sorry. I don't know what to say."

She raises her voice to just above a whisper. "Well, you need to say more than you're sorry."

Forcefully, I say, "Things just got real complicated for me."

"In three days? They weren't complicated when we were just fucking."

"Nadia, listen..."

"No, look, Laila...everything you're saying—better yet, not saying to me—is making no sense. So, I'm going to leave right now, and you can call me when you get it together."

I am absolutely floored, but I try to hide it. After grabbing her purse and phone, Nadia leaves me sitting there in tears. She storms out of the building and doesn't look back. I was expecting her to cry because she is so sensitive, but she didn't.

She's not even sad. She's mad. I didn't anticipate her getting that angry. Upset maybe, but angry? I don't know how to process it.

My head is in my hands, when Shay walks over.

"Things didn't go as planned, huh?" she says. "It's gonna be okay, though."

She rubs me on the back, and I let out a soft laugh at how this played out.

How pretentious of me to think Nadia would be tragically broken by my breaking up with her! God! What is wrong with me?

I ask Shay to bring me the bill, pay it, and leave before I embarrass myself more.

After leaving the café, I walk around DuPont Circle aimlessly for a while. After about two hours of going in and out of shops, I go into a bookstore. It may be beneficial for Victoria and me to read some parenting books, so I find a couple I think will be suitable and pull them off the shelves. When I have five in hand, I sit down on the floor of an empty aisle because all of the tables are full.

I am engrossed in one of the books, when I'm overcome with an eerie feeling. When I lift my head to glance around, Tasha sits down beside me. I scream and jump up.

"Get away from me!" I yell. "I have a restraining order!"

She tries to talk over me. "Look, Laila, I'm sorry. I wasn't on my medicine."

I look around and realize there's only one way off this aisle, and she's blocking it. I scream for help, and then I muster all the strength I have and push her out of the way. She falls backward into a round table of books, and I run toward the front door.

I burst out of the door onto Connecticut Avenue, turn right, and run at top speed for about three blocks. I hear a man's voice screaming at me to stop, but I can't. Then the voice says, "Freeze! Police!" I turn my head to look behind me and slow my pace when I see his uniform. He keeps running toward me and grabs me in a bear hug when he reaches me. He puts me on the ground, and I start crying.

He commands, "Put your hands behind your head and don't move."

"Okay, okay."

I am lying down face-to-face with the dirty cement, and people are gathering around. Through deep breaths, he asks me why I was running. I try to tell him that I was scared, but he can't understand me through the sobbing and heavy breathing.

He asks, "Look, if I sit you up, are you going to be cool?"

"Yes," I tell him.

He sits me up by the wall and grabs my messenger bag. "Lady, why were you running and screaming like a bat out of hell?"

"Because she was in there."

"Who was where? Listen, take a deep breath, and tell me what you're talking about."

I try to pull it together, as two more officers arrive on the scene.

While trying to stop crying, I tell them, "I was in the bookstore reading, and then Tasha came in there. I had to run to get away from her."

"Who is Tasha?

"Tasha Smith. I have a restraining order against her."

"So you were running away from someone who you have a restraining order against?"

"Yes."

"Do you mind getting in the back of the police car while we check this out?"

I shake my head no.

"Do you have any weapons or drugs on you?"

I say no.

The woman officer comes over, searches me, and then puts me in the squad car. It takes them about twenty minutes to check my story out. The police give me a ride back to my car and release me. Once in the car, I immediately call Tori, but she doesn't answer.

It's like déjà vu. The last time something happened with Tasha, I couldn't get in contact with Tori for days. Once I finally did, I was so upset that I didn't even bother to tell her what happened. I try calling her three more times, but she doesn't answer. I start to call Camille, but realize I can't. I scream and bang on the steering wheel in frustration before pulling off.

When I arrive home, Tori isn't there. I check the fridge for the groceries we purchased, and there is no food in sight. I pick the phone up to call her again, but just as I do, she walks through the door.

"Tori, where have you been?"

"I went to visit Christina."

I stare at her disapprovingly for a moment, then my eyes well up with tears. *I needed you.*

"Laila, what's wrong, honey?"

Anger is billowing in my stomach, but I repress it because I don't want to argue with her. I try to say to her in a composed voice that I really needed her to be there for me, but it doesn't work. The tears fall. So much has happened that we have not discussed. I express that I want our relationship to work, but we have to be able to trust each other.

"What do you mean? I do trust you," is her reply, but I still don't trust her fully.

"I mean we have to stop disappearing on each other and know that we can count on each other, Tori. I don't want to turn to anyone else for comfort, and I don't want you to either."

She stretches her arms out across the countertop. "I know, love. I want us to mend our relationship too."

"I really needed you earlier. Tasha tried to trap me in the bookstore today."

"What?"

"Yeah. She violated her restraining order."

"Restraining order?"

"I never told you about it."

"Well, can you do it now?" she asks.

Tori comes around to the other side of the counter and hugs me. I notice she smells different, but I ignore it. I take her back to the day when Tasha burst into my office with a gun.

When I'm done speaking, she becomes overly apologetic for not being here for me. She tries to reassure me that it won't happen again. She tells me that she's ready to try anything and informs me that she has made an appointment to see a therapist. I smile at that. We spend the rest of the night talking, and Tori tells me about her trip to Wisconsin. I hadn't asked her about it, and she didn't bring it up.

I get in the bed early because I plan on going into the office early. I have work I need to catch up on, and I've frequently been leaving work early these past months. That's something that has never happened in the seven years I worked for Expected Architecture. I've never taken off more than eight days in a whole year. More than likely, that's the reason they've been letting me get away with cutting out early.

23

I wait for three o'clock to arrive so I can leave work and meet Tori for our therapy appointment. She is waiting in her truck when I pull into our driveway at three-thirty. I bypass going into the house as I had planned and get into her truck. As we are driving to the office, I try to take a short nap to clear my mind. Tori wakes me by gently squeezing on my leg.

"We're here, Laila. Wake up."

I sit up and see that we are sitting outside of Dr. Rivers' office. Tori made the appointment, and I didn't ask which doctor she selected. I start rubbing my forehead with the tips of my fingers.

"Are you alright?" Tori asks.

I respond, "Yes," but I really mean no. My mind is racing a mile a minute.

Is this a setup? Shit. How did she find out I was coming here? Does she know the doctor? Did Dr. Rivers tell on me?

Tori grabs my hand and says, "It'll be okay. Come on, let's go."

Why the hell does she seem so comfortable? She has always been against seeing any kind of therapist. All I can do is face it like a woman. I made this bed.

We enter the reception area and wait for Dr. Rivers to come get us. She calls us back to her office, and the butterflies in my stomach kick into high gear. I let Tori walk down the hall in front of me so she doesn't see me trying to pull myself together. Dr. Rivers tells us to sit on the couch in her office, while she sits on the edge of her desk. I try not to look directly at her and lose myself in the replica painting of Monet's *Train in the Snow* above her head.

Dr. Rivers addresses us both, and then says to Tori, "I haven't seen you in a while. I'm glad you came back."

I pull my eyes from the picture for a moment and stare at Dr. Rivers, while trying to keep a straight face. I try to stop my mind from going into overdrive, but it's impossible. I listen to the easiness in Tori's voice while she's speaking to the doctor. When Tori stops speaking, Dr. Rivers redirects her attention to me, and I slowly move my eyes back to the picture.

I think Dr. Rivers senses my skepticism, so she asks us if we're ready to get started. We both reply yes. She starts the conversation by telling us that we need to go back to when we first started having problems.

"Tori, why don't you tell Laila about how we met."

"Laila, I met Dr. Rivers shortly after what happened happened."

Dr. Rivers says, "Tori?" as if telling her to continue.

"After I was raped, I started going to group meetings with Dr. Rivers and Christina."

I drop my head and start looking at my fingers. "When are the groups?" I ask Tori.

She responds, "Every Tuesday and Thursday."

I already knew the answer to the question. *I've been totally off base with everything.*

Then I ask Tori, "How come you never wanted to come to therapy with me?"

"I was trying to hide so much other stuff from you that I wasn't receptive to your suggestions, and I thought it would expose me."

"How do you feel now that you know a little more about what was going on, Laila?" Dr. Rivers asks.

"I feel like a fool is what I feel like. I was angry for so long and hurt because you didn't come to me, Tori."

"Laila, I was going through a lot and didn't know how to deal with it. I know sorry isn't enough, but—"

"You didn't even give me the chance to be there for you, Tori. You withdrew from me so much, and I thought..."

Dr. Rivers chimes in, "Excuse me a minute, ladies. Tori, do you understand why Laila felt so hurt?"

"Yes, a little, but I didn't know what to do."

She tells me, "Laila, try to explain how you felt. Not what you thought was going on, but how you felt."

"Tori, I felt angry, sad, alone...rejected."

Dr. Rivers asks, "What made you feel that way?"

"We've been together for years, and she just stopped talking to me. I would try to connect with her, but she kept shutting me down. I knew something was wrong, but she wouldn't say anything. Then she started being angry all the time..."

Tears begin to fall from Tori's eyes. "I'm so sorry, Laila. I'm sorry I made you feel that way."

"Laila, do you understand why it was difficult for Tori to talk to you?"

I nod my head yes.

Dr. Rivers then explains to me some of the things that rape victims go through mentally. As she is describing them, Tori's actions become clearer and clearer. I was so insensitive. I've created an absolute mess, all based off of an assumption.

I take my hand from underneath Tori's and place it on top of hers. She is looking down at her lap with her eyes closed. I look at Dr. Rivers, and she motions with her hand that it's okay. Dr. Rivers tries to reassure me that my initial reaction to Tori's behavior was warranted. Her statements do nothing to chip away the guilt I feel. I took things way too far.

Dr. Rivers asks if we want to move forward with the conversation, because she knows there is still a lot unresolved in that area, and she would like for us to put everything out on the table now, so there are no roadblocks later. My stomach starts to turn, and I become really uncomfortable. I'm not ready to tell Tori all that I've done. I begin to fidget. Tori asks if I'm all right.

"I'm okay. It's just a lot to take in."

"Laila, why don't you tell Tori why you started to come see me?"

Tori says, "I didn't know Dr. Rivers is your therapist."

"I'm surprised that you've been seeing her," I respond.

"Because of patient confidentiality, I could not disclose that both of you are my clients. I hope you understand that."

Tori responds that she is fine with it, and I force myself to say I am, but actually I'm terrified. I don't think Dr. Rivers would say anything about my other relationships, but I'm extremely nervous. I didn't plan on telling Tori about Nadia or Camille. Hopefully, everything will continue to go as smoothly as it has, and all of my lies won't come back to bite me in the ass.

The alarm on my phone goes off. I set it so I would know when the hour appointment was over.

I cut it off and apologize. "I'm sorry; I thought my phone was on silent."

After looking at the clock, I inform Dr. Rivers and Tori of the time.

"I think our hour is up, Dr. Rivers."

"Is it five o'clock already? I've cleared the next two hours on my schedule, if you all want to continue."

Please don't agree. Please say you want to go home.

"I'm okay with staying if you are, Laila."

SHHHIIIITTT, this chick is fired.

I smile and say, "I'm okay with that."

"Okay, great. Do you all want to take a break?"

I shake my head, and Tori says, "I'm okay, but do you have some water?"

Dr. River says, "Yes," then gets up and gets us each a bottle.

She settles back in her chair and asks us, "So where were we in the discussion?"

Tori reminds us that I was about to tell her why I started coming to therapy.

I give a surface level answer by telling Tori, "I was extremely hurt by you leaving the way you did, and I couldn't cope. I was breaking down and needed help pulling it together. I started getting depressed."

I look over at Dr. Rivers, who puts her fist under her chin and stares at me with a look of chastisement in her eyes.

I look at the ground and continue. "I just felt really lost and needed help pulling it together." I get choked up. "I was preparing for the end of our relationship."

Tori leans over and hugs me. "I'm here, baby. I want us to work things out. I'm not going anywhere."

"I want the same thing, Tori. I want us to get back to the way we were before."

Dr. Rivers interrupts us. "I'm glad you both want the same thing. That's important for the rebuilding process, because there is a major change about to occur in your lives."

Tori whispers, "I know."

"How do you feel about that, Laila?" Dr. Rivers asks.

"I'm totally fine with it. I just want Tori to be okay."

"So you both know for sure that you want the baby?"

I tell her, "Yes. We decided we were going to keep it on Saturday."

She calls Tori's name. When Tori looks at her, she asks, "You want the same thing as Laila?"

"Yes."

Dr. Rivers explains to us that we should keep coming to therapy together and individually; she wants us to start preparing mentally for the baby. She reassures us that what we talk to her about in our individual sessions will stay confidential. She can't risk losing her license. Then she asks if I will come to the group meeting tomorrow with Tori. I'm nervous about it, but I say I will come if Tori wants me to.

After discussing a possible schedule for our appointment, Dr. Rivers tries to direct the conversation toward my telling Tori about all that occurred while she was away. But, every time she does, I redirect the conversation.

The next two hours pass just as quickly as the first one, and our time ends without me disclosing my other relationships. A lot of ground is covered, and the doors of communication are opened up for Tori and I.

When we leave Dr. Rivers' office, I think both of us feel a lot better. A lot of the tension that was there has melted away.

Shortly after we arrive home, Tori goes to bed. She has been going to bed earlier and earlier, but I stay up to clean. I have so much on my mind. I start cleaning, and before I know it, all three floors of the house are sparkling. I get in the bed around eleven-thirty, but find myself looking at the clock until about two:ten.

Tori wakes me up at three forty-five to tell me her belly hurts. I ask if she wants to go to the hospital, but she says no. She says she will call Dr. Gray in the morning. Sleep finally calls my name, but I stay up with her until the pain subsides. After about two hours, she tells me that she is comfortable, and we go to sleep. It doesn't last long, though, because I have the most horrible dream that Tasha is attacking me.

If I keep this up, I may have to get some sleep pills.

I curl up as close to Tori as possible and wait for the sun to rise.

24

My phone rings at seven-thirty exactly. I answer it with an agitated tone. It's my job calling to tell me my driver will be coming to pick me up today, and they need to confirm a pickup time. The whole driver doubling as a bodyguard thing freaked me out, so I refused the services and I've been driving myself to work lately and frankly, I've enjoyed being in the car alone in the mornings.

Expected has never sent my driver to pick me up. So, I wonder what's going on.

Tori rolls over and asks, "Who was that?"

"My job. They're sending Shelton to pick me up at nine."

"Oh, do you want me to get up with you?"

I kiss her on the cheek. "No, try to sleep. When you get up, don't forget to call Dr. Gray, or do you want me to call him for you?"

"No, I'll do it. If I can get in to see him, I'll call to let you know what time."

Promptly at nine, my driver arrives to pick me up. Another gentleman, one who I'm unfamiliar with, accompanies him. Shelton knocks on the door. After greeting me, he tells me that the man standing at the end of the sidewalk looking around is James. He then explains that Expected Architecture has hired another bodyguard for me.

He gives me a mouthful of information before we reach the end of the sidewalk.

When we reach James, he introduces himself and tells me I can have complete confidence in him. I become extremely anxious. While on the way to the office, my stomach becomes upset, so I tell James to pull over to the side of road. He stops the car just in time for me to open the door and vomit. When I'm done, I tell him to take me back to the house so I can go refresh myself.

James makes a phone call and states we're off route and on the way back to my house. I don't know what's going on, but it must be serious.

"James, who did you call and check in with?"

"Expected has told us to keep them updated on your status."

"What's going on?" I ask.

"I'm not sure, Ms. Morriston, but the situation must be dire for them to assign you security," James comments.

"I don't feel well."

Shelton asks, "Do you need me to pull over again?"

"No, I'll be okay. Have they told you why I need extra security?"

"No, ma'am, but the security company has you listed under a code black."

"What's a code black?"

James answers, "It's the strongest security level we have, which means we will be in close proximity to you at all times."

"All the time... like full-time bodyguards?"

"Yes, ma'am. On the weekends, someone else will be with you, though."

"Why would an architecture firm hire full-time security?"

"They feel responsible."

I raise my voice at James in agitation. "Why is this necessary? How come you can't tell me anything? Shelton, what do you know?"

Shelton offers me no more of an explanation than James.

When I return home, Tori is gone. She left her cell phone on the kitchen counter, so I can't even call her. I change clothes, wash my face, brush my teeth.

At work, I go into my office and get to work on the plans I started drafting yesterday. John comes into my office and asks me if I'm feeling okay because he heard I got sick.

Does everyone know my business in this building?

I say yes, and then he tells me there's a meeting scheduled for noon and to email Sandra, the office secretary, what I would like for lunch. When I ask him what's going on, he says we'll talk about it in the meeting. He tries to reassure me that management has taken care of everything and tells me not to worry. I don't know how he expects me not to worry when I don't have any information about what's going on. Tasha held me hostage in the office, and now I have a security detail. On top of that, there are three women who are not pleased with me at the moment.

Laila, what have you gotten yourself into?

Thoughts of Nadia flood my mind after John leaves my office. She hasn't contacted me since Sunday. I'm worried about her, and as selfish as it may be, I was hoping she and I could be friends. I feel like a small part of me is missing without her. She and I mesh so well, and if I weren't already committed to Victoria, I would try to be with her indefinitely.

My phone rings four times before I pick it up. I consider not answering it, but I remember Tori is supposed to call me. Without looking at the screen, I answer it and I'm caught off guard by Camille's voice.

"Hey, sexy lady. How are you?"

In my business tone, I reply, "Hello, Camille."

"Why so formal, Laila?"

In a softened tone, I respond, "You know I'm at work."

"Okay, I won't keep you long then."

"No! I have a minute. Wassup?"

"I was thinking we could meet up so I could give you some things I picked up in New York for you."

"Camille, I'm not so sure that's a good idea."

"Why is it *not* a good idea? We can't have friendly conversation anymore?"

"No, it's not that. I just think we need more time before we start hanging out."

"Why do we need more time? We have already established we're not together, unless you're not sure about your decision."

"I just…I just don't think it is such a good idea."

"Why do you think it's not a good idea? Tell me your feelings."

"I don't want to get into all of that, Camille. I don't know what good it would do anyway."

"Look, I just have a couple of things I need to give you, that's all. I'm not going to try anything."

"I'm not worried about you trying anything, honey."

"What are you worried about then?" she asks.

"Umm… things becoming complicated."

"Laila, all I'm asking for is fifteen minutes so I can give you the stuff I got for you."

"Fifteen minutes, huh?"

"Yes, just fifteen."

"Okay. How about Friday at five?"

"That works for me."

"Okay, see you then."

"All right. Have a good day."

Once I hang the phone up, I go to the door and let Krystal in. She has been waiting outside my door for five minutes. I like the way she respects my space, instead of barging in on me. She waits until I acknowledge her, something Tasha didn't do very often. But that was my fault for not setting boundaries. When I let her in, she informs me that everyone's lunch has arrived and the meeting will start in five minutes.

As I'm walking into the meeting, my cell phone rings. It's Tori, but I can't answer it. I send her a text telling her to text me whatever it is she has to tell me. I take a seat next to John, as always. He and I like to write silly notes back and forth to each other in these meetings. The CEOs, Cory and Cassandra Bleakes, are in attendance, which means we'll probably be talking about our new hire. They only come to the meetings when major changes are about to happen with the company.

Cassandra calls the meeting to order and opens with a slideshow depicting the new vision for Expected Architecture. The company is going to expand internationally and open a site in Bangkok. Collectively, all of the architects and engineers will help design the building and landscaping for the site. Construction is supposed to start a year and a half from now. They want five of us who are currently working with the company to relocate to Bangkok at that time. I become excited and start thinking about all the possibilities.

As they wrap up the presentation, my phone vibrates. It's a text from Tori. She tells me she just left Doctor Gray's office and she's on her way home. She doesn't elaborate, which causes me to get upset. I don't understand why she didn't text me back earlier or tell me she was at the doctor's office.

Cory says my name, pulling my mind back to the meeting. He asks me to stand up, and now I really wish I hadn't let my mind drift away. Cory gives a short speech about the excellent work I've been doing, which I personally think hasn't been so great lately because of all the shit I've had going on. But he says STS Enterprises is so impressed with all the good work I've done for them that they have scheduled another project with the company. For my services, they are awarding me a bonus of $25,000. I am absolutely stunned. My mouth flies open. John pats me on the arm and says congratulations.

They tell me they want me to head the next project for STS Enterprises, instead of John, but he should plan to continue to be hands-on. John is given a bonus of $10,000, and a couple other rewards are given out before the meeting moves on. The next topic on the agenda is the hiring of Camille. Cory explains what Camille's position is going to be and that she already agreed to go to Bangkok.

That cancels that for me.

She's due to start in less than two weeks, so they ask for a volunteer to take her under their wing and help her further develop her skills. Everyone looks at me as though I was automatically going to volunteer. John says I should do it because of the excellent job I did with her when she was my intern, and because we've already built such great rapport. I want to tell him to shut up, but I reluctantly agree. The only upside to the situation is that she will be leaving in a year.

The last thing on the meeting's agenda is my situation with Tasha.

Everyone who's not in a "need to know" position is asked to leave. Detective Williams enters the meeting and gives a short brief. He tells everyone that Tasha is not allowed within five hundred feet of the building, and if anyone sees her, to report it to security immediately. He tells us that unfortunately, she hasn't been apprehended, but the authorities are looking for her. Cory chimes in and tells me the police think it's important that I have the security detail.

At first, I don't understand why they are so adamant, but Detective Williams clarifies it for me. He explains that while they've been unable to apprehend Tasha, they're aware that she's made some suspicious purchases lately. They want all of us to be wary of her and to report anything suspicious to security.

He continues by saying, "I need all of you to understand that Tasha Smith is mentally unstable. At the moment, we are unable to locate her, but an arrest warrant has been issued."

I become antsy and start squirming in my seat. I motion for Krystal to bring me some water. It seems like forever before she comes back.

One of my co-workers asks the detective, "Could you maybe tell us what she's been doing so we have a better idea of what to look for?"

Detective Williams looks at me, as if he's waiting for me to object.

I say, "Yes, please tell us things to look for."

"Well, she's bought a cargo van, a large amount of ammo, and protective gear in her grandmother's name."

"Ammo? A van?" I say.

He responds, "Yes. We have a manhunt underway to locate her, she may have mental health issues."

I rub my hand across my head.

Cassandra says to me, "Laila, we need you to make sure you listen to your security detail, okay?"

I nod and reply, "I will." I'm so nervous.

Detective Williams ends his brief by telling me he needs to speak with me privately.

After the meeting ends, I head back to my office. John tries to talk to me, but I tell him I have to call Tori because she had to go to the doctor. After he walks away, Krystal comes up and tells me that a Nadia York has called twice but left no message. I get excited and pick up my pace a little. I sit down at my desk and start dialing Nadia's number, but realize I should probably call Tori back first.

"Hey, Tori, what are you doing?"

"Nothing. Lying in the bed, about to take a nap."

"Are you okay?"

"Yes, but the doctor said it looks like I have the beginning stages of pre-eclampsia and I need to keep my stress level down, among other things."

"Honey, I wanted to go with you."

"I know, but when I called, he told me to come in right then. There wouldn't have been time for you to make it all the way back to Upper Marlboro."

"I could've tried."

"I know, babe, but..."

"You're right. It would have taken too much time, but anyway, how do you feel?"

"Okay, I suppose. Just worried."

"It's going to be all right. I promise."

"I hope so, Laila. I just can't help thinkin' it won't. I should've never taken that pill."

She sounds like she's going to cry.

"Shhh, shhh, honey. Don't think about that. Let's focus on the future."

"I'm trying to, but it's not that easy."

"I know, but we'll get through whatever comes our way."

She changes the conversation and asks if I'm going to the meeting with her later. I tell her yes. She doesn't say anything for a while, and I notice her breathing has become heavy. I want to tell her about Tasha, but I feel it will stress her out more.

Quietly, I whisper, "Sleep well, honey," and hang up the phone. Then I call Nadia. I call her three times, but she doesn't answer. I'm saddened that I can't get in contact with her and consider calling Mrs. Spady, but decide against it.

Detective Williams knocks on my door and opens it slightly.

"Come in, sir."

"I just need to talk with you for a minute. I won't take up too much of your time."

I say, "It's okay. I have a moment."

We make small talk and then he asks me to write a detailed statement as to what happened in the bookstore. I begin to write the statement for him while trying not to notice the way he's watching me. He smiles at me when I slide the statement across my desk. He gives me his card and tells me to call him if I have any questions. I take it and try to get him out of my office quickly.

For the rest of the day, I sit and try to finish as much work as possible. I think about what it would be like to live in Bangkok, but then all the other stuff I have going on overshadows those thoughts. The most prevalent issue is that I have a baby on the way. Tori and I have so much to do in so little time. I have to wrap my head around the fact that we're going to have a disabled child and I truly don't know how Victoria is going to react to everything.

I glance at the clock and realize it's time for me to leave. I try calling Nadia again, but she still doesn't answer.

I call my security detail to take me home. It's weird having people follow me around. When I get there, I find Tori still sleeping. I wake and rush her to get dressed. We make it to the group therapy place five minutes before the meeting starts. I grab Tori's hand as we walk through the door and realize she's nervous.

"Baby, are you okay?" I ask her.

"Why do you ask that?"

"Because your palm is sweaty."

"Oh… No, I'm fine. Just a little hot, that's all."

Tori and I walk into the room, and the first person I notice is Christina. She smiles really big when she sees Tori, but then frowns when she sees me. I look over at Tori, who's looking at the floor.

There's a seat next to Christina with a bag on it. Christina snatches the bag up and puts it in her lap. I lead

Victoria toward two open chairs directly across from Christina. She tries to pull me in another direction, but I don't let her. Just as we're about to sit down, Dr. Rivers comes in and calls my name. I turn to look at her and see that she's waving her hand for me to come to her.

"Can you come here, please? I have something for you."

I give Tori my purse and walk over to her.

She tells me she's glad I'm at the meeting and she gives me a quick overview of the group rules and so forth. Then she hands me a book on partners of sexual abuse survivors. Dr. Rivers asks me not to say much, because normally this meeting is closed to the victims, but everyone has agreed that I can attend for Tori's sake. I shake my head in agreement, then she tells me that I need to know Christina has helped Tori through some difficult times. I fully understand why she says this to me, but I still can't help but feel hurt and angry that Tori didn't give me a chance to help her.

The meeting starts, and I try not to make eye contact with Christina, but I can't help it. Every now and again, I catch her looking at Tori. I try to ignore it, but she's making me jealous. I keep thinking something has been or is going on between them.

Tears pour from my eyes as I listen to the things people in the group have been through and are struggling with. Tori places her hand on my knee, trying to comfort me. While in the meeting, I realize how blind and selfish I've been these past eight months. I become emotional and begin to think about how tragic things could have been. I can't imagine my life without Tori. I wanted to think I would have been okay and could have gotten over us breaking up, but the truth is, she means everything to me.

I don't know why I've been so foolish. I don't want to be with anyone but Tori, and I've felt this way for years. There were times when I really should have left her, but I didn't. I decided to work it out, and I'm going to do that now.

I love her more than she will ever know.

The meeting ends, and Tori and I leave quickly. I want to talk to Dr. Rivers, but Tori says she isn't feeling well and wants to get home. After we get in the car, Tori thanks me for going to the meeting with her, and I apologize to her for the way I've been acting.

Tori looks at me with tears in her eyes and says, "I love you."

I become overwhelmed because I want to spend the rest of my life with her. I tell Tori to pull the car over. When we park, I get out, walk over to her side of the car, and ask her to get out. Shelton and James are about to get out of their car, but I ward them off.

Once she's out of the car, I get down on one knee and ask her, "Will you marry me?"

She doesn't say anything for a moment and then asks, "Are you serious, Laila?"

"Yes! Will you marry me?"

She leans back onto the car, looks at me, and says, "Yes! Wow! Yes!"

I start to scream while jumping up and down. I honestly wasn't expecting her to say yes. She hugs me and asks if I'm sure about this.

I tell her, "Yes. I want to be with you forever. You're the only person I am in love with."

The rest of our night goes extremely well. We stand in the parking lot and talk for hours before going home and making love for the first time in what seems like forever. It's different having sex with a pregnant woman. I felt like I needed to be more careful.

25

When I wake up, I'm on top of the world. I feel like there's nothing that can take my joy away. I make Tori breakfast and arrange to go into work late so I can go find an engagement ring. Right before I leave the house, Tori wakes up and comes downstairs. We sit and talk for two hours, then I bolt out of house to go get her ring.

I visit eight different stores before finding a ring I think she will like. I am ecstatic; then, in the blink of an eye, my world stops spinning. I ask the jeweler to turn up the radio when I hear the DJ say my name. I am in disbelief.

I ask, "Did he just say Laila Morriston?"

She responds, "I think so."

I laugh and say, "No, he didn't just say that. There's no way."

Then he says it again. "If your name is Laila Morriston, please get down to H Street now."

My phone starts ringing. I stick my hand in my purse and hit ignore, but it rings again. I pull the phone out and look at the screen. It's Detective Williams. Shelton and James burst into the store and tell me that we have to go now. I almost forgot they were following me. I try to get information out of them, but all Shelton keeps saying is that we have to go. I start to panic and ask him if something is wrong with Tori.

He tells me, "No. It's Tasha."

As they pull me out of the door, I ask the sales clerk to hold the ring for me. She nods and looks at me with a confused expression. I feel the way her face looks.

James calls Detective Williams and tells him we're on our way. Again, I press James for information, but he doesn't have many details. All they know is that Tasha has barricaded herself on top of the Verizon Center, and my presence is pertinent. I feel like I'm going to pass out. Shelton tries to calm me, but it doesn't work. I hear fire trucks in the distance and see helicopters flying overhead.

"What is going on?" I yell, but they don't respond.

After the car abruptly stops, two officers usher me to a SWAT Team truck. Once inside, I sit down and start to hyperventilate. Everything is happening so quickly!

A paramedic comes up to me and gives me water. I take a big swig from the bottle, spilling some of the water on my shirt. My phone rings, and I start to answer it, but someone tells me not to. There's so much going on around me, but I block it out. People are scrambling, but it's silent and still. I take another drink, then ask if someone can tell me what's going on. My phone rings again, and it's Trey. Someone calls my name while I'm looking at the screen. I look up, and it's Detective Williams. I stand up and hug him reflexively. I don't know why, maybe because I'm scared. He tells me to sit down and begins to answer the question I've been asking everyone repeatedly: What is going on?

"Ms. Morriston," he begins, "Tasha has climbed up on the roof and barricaded herself. She is threatening to kill herself and others."

I know I did not hear him correctly.

"Excuse me? She did what?"

"Climbed on the roof—"

"Why did they say my name on the radio?"

"Ms. Morriston, she said that in order to save innocent victims, she wants to see you."

"No, I can't."

"She probably will be fine once she sees you."

"How did she even manage to get up there?"

"I don't know, but what we do know is that she's holding a sign that says only you can save her."

"What the fuck! She is certifiable."

"She really is. Also, it has not been confirmed, but she appears to be holding an AK-47. We are unable to determine the extent of her threats or what her plans are, so we are taking extreme caution. She doesn't want to negotiate until she sees you."

"She has a what? Wait! You want me to put myself in harm's way?"

"We have people in place if she tries anything."

They turn on the monitors in the truck, and I can see Tasha pacing back and forth on the roof.

I scream at him, "How did this happen? How was she able to do this?"

"Please calm down, Ms. Morriston. We've been looking for her, but couldn't find her. But you can be sure that after this stunt, she's going to go to jail with no bail this time. I guarantee you won't have to worry about her anymore."

I laugh at him condescendingly. "No disrespect, but I've heard that before."

He squints then says he has to check on things and will be right back. I pick my phone up, and I'm about to call Tori, but before I can, Nadia calls me. I ask if I may answer the phone and I'm given the go-ahead. While talking to Nadia, all I can think about is whether Tori's okay. She and the baby don't need any more stress. Nadia tells me that she's on her way down to meet me. About ten minutes go by, and Detective Williams still hasn't come back. So much is going on around me that I decide to focus on the monitors to steady my mind.

I see Nadia walk up and join the small crowd that's forming. I get up and go to the screen to get a better view. I ask the officer if he can pan back over that part of the crowd so I can confirm it's her. He asks me if I know her. I tell him yes, and he asks if I would like someone to go get her. That surprises me, so I ask him if that's okay. He tells me that in a crisis like this, it's good to have someone around who can calm you down.

I say, "That would be wonderful."

He has a short conversation with Detective Williams, and they dispatch someone to get her from the crowd.

Nadia is brought inside the trailer, and we talk for a while until Detective Williams comes over. He tells me they need me to go outside because Tasha needs to see that I'm on the scene. They strap a bulletproof vest to me, put some type of heavy-duty helmet on my head, and have me put on a pair of pants that feel like they have lead in them. After Detective Williams puts on one of the helmets, we exit the trailer.

Once outside, I see they have set up a jump cushion on the sidewalk in front of the Verizon Center and adjacent stores. A SWAT helicopter is hovering overhead, with someone hanging from a bungee-type cord. The person is right in front of Tasha and pointing down at the ground. Detective Williams tells me to wave to her. Inside, I'm saying, *Hell no,* but I raise my left arm and sway it back and forth.

This is humiliating. News stations are everywhere, hundreds of safety personnel, the crowd is continually growing, and now I am being forced to wave to this crazy bitch! My life has turned into a horrible train wreck!

26

Laila's Women

Camille

I'm sitting at my desk when Jeremy tells me that Laila is on TV. After watching the broadcast for about two minutes, the woman I've been in love with for the past six months appears.

"Come on, Jeremy. Grab your jacket *now*. We have to go."

I drop him off at his father's house and make it to Chinatown in about twenty minutes. I try to get as close as possible to the Verizon Center, but I'm stopped in front of the Gallery Place/Chinatown metro entrance. I make my way through the crowd until I'm right behind the yellow caution tape. I ask the gentleman next to me if anything has happened. He tells me no and then says while pointing, "I think that's the Laila woman over there." I see Laila standing there in SWAT gear with a pair of heels on. My heart rate speeds up and my palms become sweaty. A news camera zoomed in on her face shows her mascara is running down her cheeks. Laila's arms are folded, and she's rocking back and forth.

Just before she bends over to take off her four-inch heels, she turns and looks in my direction like she knows

I'm here. Remembering I have a pair of her running shoes in my trunk, I go retrieve them. When I come back, I have to convince the police that I'm her assistant so they'll let me through with her shoes. As I'm walking towards her, there's a commotion above us, so I look up. The police are apprehending Tasha.

When I look back down and spot Laila again, numerous people are surrounding her, and the officer stops me from going over to her. The person who stands out the most is the woman standing next to her, the one holding her hand. She wasn't there before. Their fingers are intertwined in a way that lets me know they're more than familiar.

I call Laila's name, and she turns her head in my direction and scans the crowd. I call her name again and our eyes lock. When they meet, she says my name in that shocked way you do when someone catches you off guard. Laila lets go of the woman's hand, takes the face shield and helmet off, then rubs her hand across her short, wavy hair. I hold out her running shoes so she can see them, prompting her, and five officers to walk towards me. I try to move closer to her, but the officer continues to block my way. When she reaches me, I hand her the shoes, grab her hand, and tell her I love her. For a moment, she tries to pull it away, but I don't let it go until she tells me she loves me back. Eventually, she whispers it, barely moving her mouth when she does. She says it nonetheless. After she tells me, I walk to the back of the crowd. I can't let her continue to break my heart.

* * *

Tori

My phone rings, and it's my friend Christina calling to tell me that someone is about to jump from the basketball arena and only Laila Morriston can save her.

"Get off my phone, Chris."

"No, Tori, I'm dead serious. I'm watching the news. OMG, they just showed her picture. Yep, that's her super wavy hair, oval face, almond-shaped eyes, and full lips."

"Okay, I got it. What channel?"

"Two."

I hang the phone up and try to call Laila. She answers on the second ring and immediately starts talking.

"Honey, I can't talk right now."

"I'm coming down there. I'll be there soon."

"No. You're in no condition to come here. I'm fine. I'll be home soon."

"What's going on, Laila?"

"Sweetie, please. I don't have time for questions right now. Stay in the house, and I mean it. Don't come down here. I love you."

"Okay, fine."

She hangs up on me, and I immediately call Christina back.

"Chris, can you please come over and get me?"

"I'm already on my way."

I turn all the TVs in the house to different news stations and get dressed while waiting for Christina to arrive.

A man being interviewed said he saw a woman walking back and forth with an assault rifle, and then she pinned a sign to the side of the building that read, *Only Laila Morriston can save me.*

"Police authorities have blocked off Chinatown, the area surrounding the Verizon Center, and have also evacuated businesses in the vicinity," the broadcaster reported. "The assailant seems to be focused only on a person by the name of Laila Morriston, who we've been told is on the scene. We will continue with updates on this situation, which will hopefully be ending soon."

Twenty minutes later, Christina arrives and rushes into the house. "Girl, what happened?" she asks.

"They got her down."

"What's wrong, Tori? You're... I don't know, but I'm getting a weird vibe."

I walk her into the living room and rewind the DVR to Laila holding hands with another woman.

"Oh," says Christina. "Well, that could be her co-worker whose hand she's holdin'. She is a femme, and Laila doesn't like feminine women, right?"

I start to cry, then fast-forward a couple of seconds to a woman telling Laila that she loves her and Laila saying it back. She mumbled it, but she definitely told the woman that she loved her.

"Who is that?"

"That woman is a stud, Chris. How do you explain that? I... I..."

I start to hyperventilate, so Christina finds a bag for me to breathe into.

"Calm down, Tori. Don't get too worked up, honey."

* * *

Nadia

While riding around DuPont Circle, the radio DJ interrupts my song to make a special announcement.

"If your name is Laila Morriston, please get down to H and Seventh ASAP. Again, if your name is Laila Morriston, please get down to the Verizon Center now."

I know they did not just say who I think they did.

The radio announcer goes on to apologize to listeners for interrupting the broadcast, but he says there is breaking news. "There is a woman holed up on top of the Verizon Center who's calling out Laila Morriston. There's a sign that reads: *Only Laila Morriston can save me.* So, if you are or know Laila Morriston, please get her to the Verizon

Center ASAP. You can't write true-life, people. You can't write true-life."

I park my car in the nearest parking garage and call Laila. After an eternity, she answers.

"Laila, where are you? Have you heard?"

"I can't talk right now. I have to go."

"Well, I'm on my way down there, okay?"

She hangs the phone up.

I get out of my car and run to the main level of the garage, then to the nearest Metro station and catch the train to the Metro Center station. I run four blocks up F Street to Eighth. The media is congregating along with a handful of spectators.

An officer approaches me. I tell him that I'm Laila's lover when he questions if I know her. They take me to the truck Laila's in. We're able to sit and talk for a little while before they whisk her away to deal with Tasha's crazy ass. I knew something was wrong with her when I met her.

After about thirty minutes, SWAT personnel move in to get Tasha down. After they have secured Tasha, an officer comes in and asks if I want to go outside to be with Laila. I tell him yes. As soon as I get close enough, I grab her hand for reassurance.

Someone from the crowd calls out Laila's name. She looks to the left, and then abruptly lets my hand go. She looks back at me with a sincere facial expression. I watch her run over to the person and grab a pair of shoes. As Laila is trying to walk away, the woman grabs her hand and says what looks like the words *I love you*. I can't really tell from this distance, but that's sure what it looked like. Eventually, she lets go of Laila's hand. When Laila turns her back, the woman bends over, wipes her hands across her face, and then walks away.

I ask Laila, "Is that Camille?"

"Yes. She brought my shoes."

"Oh. Did she—" I stop myself from asking a question I really don't want the answer to.

The police walk over and take us back to the SWAT truck. Laila keeps a safe distance between us as we are walking. Once inside the truck, a detective informs us that Tasha is on her way to jail.

I place my hand on top of Laila's and say, "It's over, honey. Everything will be all right."

She fake smiles and bites her lip and tries to hold back tears. Her demeanor has changed. She seems more disconnected from what's going on, more so than before. She pulls her hand away from me and starts rubbing her hands together. The detective is still talking to us, but her mind seems to be somewhere else. Frantically, she begins stripping out of the gear they put on her. Detective Williams is trying to talk to her, but she interrupts him and asks if she can leave. He says he doesn't have the authority to let her leave.

Laila stands up, looks at him, then me and says, "I'm sorry Nadia, but I have to go. I love you." Then she walks toward the door.

The detective calls her name but she ignores him.

He asks me, "Is she okay?"

"I don't know. Sometimes she just likes to be alone."

"Oh."

As I get up to leave, he follows me outside. We see Laila surrounded by the press. We run over and rescue her from the madness. A couple more officers come over and help us make our way through the crowd. Once we are clear, Detective Williams comes over and tries to get Laila back in the truck, but she says she needs to leave. After five minutes of going back and forth, he decides to let her go. He walks us over to two officers leaning against their cruisers. Laila looks at me with tearful eyes, and I say what she doesn't want to.

"We need both of the cars."

I reluctantly make our departure quick.

27

Things in my life just got real bad real fast. The fiasco with Tasha has turned into a nightmare. Camille and Nadia showed up on the scene, and there were dozens of cameras around. Who knows what they captured? I am so foolish. I care about them and their feelings so much that I let things get way out of hand. I shouldn't have gotten caught up with either of them.

Nadia appeals to the part of me that likes to party and explore different things, like poetry readings. She knows how to calm me down, like Tori used to do, but it's different with her. Her coming to be with me was great, but I may have given her the wrong impression about where we are in our relationship. I'm not sure if she took my breaking up with her seriously. I was aware that cameras were around, but I ignored them and held hands with her in public. The fact that Tori might see us didn't cross my mind, until Camille called my name. When I heard her yell, I knew immediately it was her, but I couldn't see her. She startled me, and I let go of Nadia's hand with a quickness.

She brought me a pair of my running shoes, and after giving them to me, forced me into saying I love her. We should've never started saying that to each other. She grabbed my hand and would not let it go. I knew the only way she would leave was if I said the words back to her.

Camille challenges the intellectual side of me. We've always had the most interesting conversations, and she and I do a lot of cultural things together. We visited a lot of museums and different ethnic restaurants when we weren't having sex.

An officer escorts me away from Chinatown back to my office building. I get into the car with Shelton and James, who I ask to take me back to the store. We pull up to the jewelry store, but I am unable to get out of the car. I break down crying. Shelton offers to go in and buy it for me, but I opt to do it myself. I pull myself together as much as I can and put my sunglasses on. I walk into the jewelry store so I can buy Tori's ring and get home as soon as possible. The sales associate who was helping me before rushes up to me. Before she can say anything, I let her know I'm in a hurry, so we need to complete this purchase quickly. Her expression changes to a more serious one. She asks me if I want to open a charge account with them. I tell her no. Then she asks me if I want to look at any other rings. I shake my head no. She walks to the back of the store and comes back with the ring. I take it out and begin to look at it again.

While I'm inspecting it, she asks, "Which of the women is the ring for? The short- or long-haired one?"

I raise my head up and look at her. "What did you ask me?"

She looks at me nervously. "I'm sorry for being intrusive."

"No, what did you ask me?"

She hesitantly repeats her question. "Which of the women is the ring for?"

"What do you mean?"

"Well, I saw you holding hands with that long-haired woman, but you said I love you to the other one."

Oh, my! If she saw that, Tori probably did, too. I begin to cry.

"Oh, Ms. Morriston, I didn't mean to… I'm sorry. Please stop crying."

I fan my eyes to dry them. "Can I just pay for the ring and leave?"

"Yes. Would you like to open an account with us?"

"I told you no already."

"I'm sorry, I'm sorry. Calm down. I didn't mean to upset you."

"Just take the card and charge it already," I demand.

"Okay, okay."

God, please let everything work out between Tori and me.

The sales associate stands there for a moment, looking at me like I'm going to change my mind.

I leave the store and try to call Tori, but she doesn't answer. After calling her three times, I decide not to call anymore and come up with a game plan. I need to figure out how I'm going to explain this pile of shit I'm in.

I don't know why I thought all of this would end well. Like they say, what starts in chaos ends in chaos.

My phone rings, and it's Trey. I've ignored all of his calls today. In fact, I haven't talked to him in a couple of days.

"Hey, Trey."

When he responds, I can barely hear him through the phone.

"Trey, speak up. I can't hear you."

He continues to whisper, but I hear him say, "Tori is at my house right now."

"What?"

"Tori is at my house. Get here now." He hangs the phone up before I can say anything.

I try to clear my mind as I'm taken to Trey's house. I want to prolong the drive, but for Trey's sake, I don't. When we pull up in front of his house, Matt is standing outside on the porch drinking a beer. He comes up to the car to greet me. After telling him I'm all right, I ask him how long Tori has been here. He tells me about an hour. He pushes his drink toward me, and I happily take it. I normally don't drink beer—or drink after other people, for that matter—but right now, I need some form of alcohol. After I tell Shelton and James to wait outside, I take a deep breath and walk through the door.

Tori's back is to me, and Trey is facing me. He takes a deep breath when I walk through the door, causing Tori to turn around. She immediately tears into me.

She screams, "How could you, Laila? How could you?"

Before walking into the house, I did not know how I was going to explain all of this, but as she fires questions at me, I immediately make my mind up. I'm going to answer any question she asks truthfully.

I run over to her, drop to my knees, and say, "Honey, I can explain."

"Stand up, Laila. Don't grovel."

I compose myself and sit down on the floor. "Tori, I'm sorry."

"So, how long have you been cheating on me?"

"I... I—"

"Stop stuttering, Laila. How long?"

Her condescension throws me off, and I lose it for a split second. But that second is too long.

"I don't know," I yell.

"You don't know? What do you mean you don't know? What—has it been years?"

"No, it hasn't been years."

"So, you do know how long?"

"A couple of months, I guess."

"You guess?"

"Tori, I'm sorry. I didn't mean for it to happen."

"But you let it happen."

"Things were just so crazy, and I thought... I thought—"

"That you could get away with it."

"No! That's not it!"

Then she asks me the explosive question. "Did you fuck both of them?"

I don't say anything. She lets out one of those I-don't-believe-this laughs, sits down on the couch, and then asks, "What's the name of the one you said I love you to?"

Trey gets up and walks out of the room.

Before I can answer, she says, "Trey tried to tell me he doesn't know anything, but I have a hard time believing that."

"Tori, can we go home and talk about this?"

"Don't try to change the subject. Is she Nadia?"

"No."

"So the other one is Nadia then?"

"Yes."

"Do you love her, too?"

"I'm in love with you, Tori, and only you."

I know I'm wrong, but a part of me feels like she is being hypocritical.

She jumps up from the couch and screams at the top of her lungs. "Then why the fuck did you tell that bitch you love her on national fucking TV?"

Trey comes back into the room and tells Tori to calm down. I stand up and try to hug her, but she pushes me away. Trey tells me to stop trying to hug her so she can calm down.

She asks me again, "Why did you tell her that you love her?"

"So she would go away."

"Bullshit! Y'all look like y'all say it to each other all the time."

She's right, but I never meant it the way Camille did.

Tori asks Trey if he can get her a glass of water because she doesn't feel well. I tell her I didn't mean for any of this to happen, that things just spiraled out of control. Tori's face tightens, and she sits down again. Almost immediately after sitting down, she falls backwards. I call her name while simultaneously running over to the couch. She's unconscious, but breathing. I scream for Trey to call an ambulance. Trey runs into the living room and asks what happened. I begin to cry. He runs over and pushes the ambulance button on the alarm system.

"I don't know. Just call an ambulance now."

Matt, Shelton, and James come into the house and ask if everything is okay. I start screaming Tori's name frantically, asking her to wake up. Matt grabs me, puts me in an armchair, and tells me to stay there. Then he instructs Trey to get the ottoman so they can prop Tori's feet up. Shelton calls 911 while James tries to wake Tori up. My panic level increases, and I start to take short, deep breaths. Matt turns around, looks at me, and tells me that I need to calm down. Trey runs into the bathroom and returns with two wet washcloths. He gives one to James and brings the other over to me.

"Put this on your head," he says to me. "I'm going to go get your inhaler."

My inhaler? I haven't had to use it in almost a year.

While Trey is talking to me, I hear James say, "Tori, honey, it's okay. Stay still, okay?"

She starts screaming and kicking at him. I jump up from the chair and run over to Tori.

"Baby, calm down. You're okay. You're okay. It's me… Laila."

It takes a moment for her to compose herself. When she does, I kiss her hand and praise the Lord. I would not be able to take it if something happened to her. The paramedics arrive after what seems like an eternity and take us to the hospital. I ride with Tori, while the guys follow us. We are at the hospital for hours waiting for tests to be run. I try to make sense of the day with Shelton, while Trey and Matt fall into their own world. Today was supposed to be a good day.

Someone turns on the television in the waiting room and breaks the silence. Secretly, I was hoping no one would turn it on. I need the silence to clear my head. The news is on, and the scene shows a recap of what happened today. My life's events are being replayed over and over again for the world to see. Splashed across the screen is this face of mine, one I hardly even recognize anymore. The woman sitting across from me looks at the screen and then at me. I call Trey's name and mouth to him that I will be right back. While making my way to the nurse's station, I run into Dr. Gray.

"Laila, I was about to come find you."

"Oh, Dr. Gray, is she going to be okay?"

"Yes, come on. Let's go see her. You've had an interesting day, haven't you, young lady?"

"I know. I don't know if I can take anything else happening."

Dr. Gray walks me to where Tori is lying on her side. I call her name when I enter the room. She doesn't turn over, but acknowledges my presence. Dr. Gray asks her to sit up so he can talk with us. I ask her if I can sit beside her on the gurney. She shrugs her shoulders, letting me know she doesn't care either way.

Dr. Gray closes the curtain and begins to deliver the not-so-good news. He tells us that Tori has pre-eclampsia and will have to be on bed rest for the rest of the pregnancy. She also needs to begin weekly steroid injections. We'll have to go visit Dr. Gray every couple of days until Tori goes into labor. He tells Tori that they still need to do a couple more things with her, and then she will be released. I kiss her on the forehead, and then Dr. Gray and I leave the room and head toward the waiting room.

While walking, Dr. Gray gives me some instructions that Tori should follow, just in case she decides not to. He asks me how I'm doing, and after a short conversation, he asks me if I would like for him to write me a prescription for some anxiety medicine. I take the prescription from him and go talk to Trey and Matt. I let them know everything is okay, and Tori will be out in a minute. It takes thirty minutes before they release her.

All of us are silent on the ride to Trey's house. I ask Tori if she wants me to drive her home, but she refuses. She asks me to go to the store and get her some strawberries. When I get home, she's sleeping in the middle of the bed, my signal to sleep somewhere else. There used to be a point in time when we worked out our problems before we went to sleep, regardless of the situation. Now we're divided, and I'm continuously adding fuel to the fire that separates us.

28

My phone rings at seven o'clock. It's John telling me we have a mandatory meeting at nine. This snowball is turning into an avalanche. I had not planned on leaving Tori today, but it may be for the best.

I need to fix things between us. I'm on the brink of losing her over things I could have controlled.

What I'm going to do is tell her everything that happened. If I hide anything, I know we will not make it. There's no need to run from my problems anymore.

I walk over to the main bedroom where Tori is sitting naked on the bed and staring out the balcony doors. Her back is to me. The cornrows she normally wears have been taken out. The scar that was so visible seven months ago is no longer there. The physical scar that launched me on a path of destruction, the physical scar that was nothing compared to the emotional and mental scars she presently has, is now gone. She takes a deep breath, with a long exhale. I call her name softly, but it startles her. She doesn't answer me.

All I can do is say, "I'm sorry."

"Don't say that," she replies.

"I have to go to work. We have a mandatory meeting."

"Will you be gone all day?"

"I don't know."

"Okay, well, have a good day, Laila."

"Can I come give you a hug?"

She shakes her head no.

"I love you, Tori."

She does not respond.

* * *

The hallways are quiet at work. Not many people are here, mainly just assistants. Krystal is standing by my door with a greeting card. We go into my office, and she asks me how I'm doing. She tells me that the Bleakes are on their way to the office. Everyone except a few select individuals have paid time off for the day. I open the card and see it's from Camille's parents.

"Umm... Krystal, can you go get me a cappuccino?"

"Yes, Ms. Morriston."

I read the card.

From the parents of Camille Jerkins-Borders. We are not sure what kind of relationship you have with our daughter—for her to make a fool of herself on national television—but it would be in your best interest to no further contact with her. Find Jesus.

Mr. and Mrs. Jerkins

I'm stunned. *Find Jesus? Wow! Camille pursued me!*

I have my head down on the table when Krystal walks in with my coffee. She tells me the meeting starts in five minutes. When I enter the conference room, John, Melissa, the public relations consultant, and Chris, the attorney, are already waiting. Cory and Cassandra have not arrived yet. I smile and greet everyone, but I want to turn around and run.

As soon as Cassandra and Cory enter the room, the small talk stops.

Cassandra looks around and says, "So, people, we could potentially have a major PR problem on our hands. We need to get everything out on the table and come up with a game plan, even if it takes all day."

Cory leans over and whispers in Chris's ear. Chris nods, then Cory states, "I'd like for us to speak frankly in this meeting today and keep everything totally confidential. Is everyone okay with that?"

We all reply yes, and then Chris passes out a confidentiality agreement to sign. After they are collected, Cory loosens his tie before lighting into me.

"Laila, what the fuck were you thinking? You may have gotten us into hot water."

John grabs my hand under the table.

"I know, I know. I'm sorry. Things just happened."

"Excuse my brother, Laila," Cassandra says. "It's just that we want to know how it is that you ended up so involved with both a client and an intern."

I begin to cry.

"John, go get some tissue," Cory says.

I respond, "It's a long story and kind of unbelievable."

Melissa says, "We've got all day."

"Laila, we're not out to get you," Cory tells me. "You're one of our best architects, but you have put us in a tight spot."

"I know. I didn't mean to. I could have done more to stop it, but—"

Chris interrupts, "Laila, we need you to be completely honest about everything, and be as accurate as possible so we can be prepared to deal with any possible backlash."

I take a deep breath and begin my story. Their jaws hit the floor when I tell them how I met Camille in a strip club. Everything else I was completely oblivious to because she didn't tell me she was in architecture school. It takes me about three hours to cover my relationship with her. There's so much that happened, so much I tried not to think about, feelings I tried to suppress and ignore but that finally surfaced. I don't want to feel anything for Camille, but I do.

I feel like a fool telling these people—my colleagues— all of my business. I've always been so good at keeping my personal life separate from work. I need to keep my job, though. I don't know if I'll be able to find another one after this debacle. They're all staring me down, judging me, but right now, that's not important. Putting my life back together is.

Everyone asks me a bunch of questions, like interrogators. I tell them what they want to know, and I realize there's so much I don't know about Camille. I hardly know anything about her parents or how she grew up, and I've never met any of her friends.

After four hours, we take a short restroom break. I walk to my office and chastise myself aloud. I can't believe I've put myself in this situation. I've always minded my p's and q's, always been so structured.

"Ms. Morriston?" Krystal appears in the doorway.

"Hmm?"

"Are you all right?"

"Yes."

"Is everything okay?"

"Yes!"

"Do you want me to stop asking you questions?"

"Yes!"

"Okay, but I do need to tell you... I saw Ms. Jerkin-Borders earlier."

"Really? Where?"

"On the elevator. She got off on the exec floor."

"Okay. Keep an eye out for her and text me anything you find out. Do me a favor, also. Call Trey and see if he's checked on Tori yet." I pull out my phone, check my messages, and then head back to the conference room to complete the second half of my story.

The story of Nadia and me isn't as complicated as the one with Camille, but it's more emotional. I tell everyone that I tried to pull away from and avoid her, but we kept ending up together. Outside all the craziness that was going on, she and I had a beautiful relationship. As an isolated entity, our relationship was close to perfect. But nothing is ever perfect, is it?

In the middle of my story, Cory asks me, "Are you in love with Nadia?"

I look at him and begin to cry. "I love Tori and only Tori."

But, that's not true. I love them all equally. How is that possible?

Cassandra says, "This is a very complicated situation."

I blow my nose.

"Listen, Laila, I want you to take some time off while we figure this mess out."

"But—"

Someone starts knocking on the door frantically; it's Krystal.

"Ms. Morriston, Tori's in the hospital."

"What! Which one?"

"Prince George's."

I jump up and look around. Cory tells me to go ahead and leave. I run to my office, grab my purse, and dash to the parking garage. I'm fumbling through my purse searching for my keys, when Camille walks up to me.

Shit. I don't need this right now.

She asks me, "Are you all right?"

"Sorry, I can't talk. I've got to go to the hospital. Tori is..."

"Huh?"

I yell and start to jump up and down. "I have to go to the hospital, and I can't find my keys!"

"Let me help you."

"No, I got it."

"Laila, let me look." She looks through my purse, but can't find them either.

I must have left them in the office.

"Let me take you," Camille offers.

"No!"

"Look, I heard you when you said where you're going. I'll drop you off and leave. I'm not into making a scene. I've done enough of that."

Tears roll down my face. "I can't. This is so messed up."

"Listen, I promise I won't make a scene."

"Camille, I can't."

"It's the least you can do, considering..." She grabs my hand in that way she does to let me know she's being sincere.

"Look, Laila, we're wasting time. Let's go."

She's right. What am I doing? Lord, please let everything be all right.

Camille and I get into her truck, and the tension is thick. We're sitting in silence, so I start watching the clock. I break the ice by asking about Jeremy. We talk about him for a little while, and then silence again. Maybe silence is better. Hopefully, I can make it out of this situation without talking about what has happened.

Fifteen minutes pass, and then she begins to speak. She starts by telling me it makes no difference to her whether I respond to what she has to say or not. She just wants to get it off her chest and then move on with her life.

Interrupting her, I say, "I know sorry isn't enough, and I didn't mean for this to happen. I do care for you, love you. You know that, right?"

"I don't know anything, Laila. But, I have stuff I need to say, and I need you to listen."

"Okay."

"I want you to know that I'm not mad at you or the situation. I'm disappointed because I ignored the signs that there was someone else. All of them were there, just as plain as day, but I ignored 'em. So, that's on me."

"Cam, I'm sorry."

"Yes, you should be, but it's not all your fault. I was so caught up in you that I blinded myself to what was right there. I wanted to be with you so badly that I ignored all the red flags. And they were there, bright as day."

"Camille, I—"

"No… let me finish. I let go of all of my reservations when it came to you. Things I've been holding back for years, and look what happened? So, I'm not mad at you, and I want to let this go because we have a long road in front of us. I was beside myself the other day, but I guarantee it will not happen again. One good thing that has come out of this is that my mother, who has not talked to me in years, called me."

"I didn't mean to hurt you, Cam."

"Man, I just wish I knew why you strung me along like a… like a puppet."

"Because you make me feel whimsical."

"Dang it, Laila. That was rhetorical."

"Oh, sorry."

"Whimsical? What does that mean? What? Young? I made you feel young? You're four years older than me."

"No, I didn't mean…"

"Yes, you did. That's exactly what you meant."

"Cam, honey…"

"You know what? I want to change the conversation. 'Cause at the end of the day, this conversation won't matter anyway because we have nothing."

"I love you, Camille."

"No, you don't."

"I do."

"How can you love me and be involved with other people?"

"Because you're a wonderful person."

"Oh, wait. I get it. I took it the wrong way. You love me, but you're not *in* love with me."

"Camille, can I be honest?"

"There's no reason not to be. Honesty is all I ever wanted from you."

"A part of me is in love with you. When I met you, I was single. Then a bunch of crazy stuff happened and I got you and others involved in this web of... of—"

"But why didn't you just let me go?"

"Because I couldn't."

"No, you're just a selfish..." Her voice drops to a whisper. "Bitch."

In shock, I suck in air. She hardly ever curses. It's true, though. Even now, I'm partially lying to her.

"I'm sorry, Laila. I didn't mean that."

She's right. I'm a selfish bitch, just like Tasha said.

"I didn't want to hurt you, so I just let things progress more and more."

"Well, things are worse now than they would've been had you let me go then. But it doesn't matter. I'm going to be all right."

"Camille, if I could fix this, I would."

"You only want to fix it 'cause you got caught."

"Dammit, Camille!"

"Well, it's true. But, like I said, let's move on, Laila, because we have to work together."

"Do you think that will be possible?"

"It's going to have to be. I already assured Expected that they wouldn't have to worry about anything from me."

Thank God! I thought she was going to hang me out to dry. But, it doesn't mean she won't.

"Camille, you're my friend, right?"

"Laila, we can't be friends. What would make you think we could?"

I don't have a response, so I sit in silence.

At the hospital, I get out the car and Camille drives away before I can walk around to the driver's side. I tried to give her a hug before I got out, but she didn't let me. Trey is calling me, but I don't answer. I need to pull my thoughts together before I talk to him. After calming myself, I walk up to the receptionist desk, get the information on Tori, and begin making my way to the maternity ward.

Trey calls me again. When I answer, he begins to ramble. "Laila, I called her numerous times, but she didn't answer. So, I came over here, but she had left. I found a note that said she was going to the hospital, but it doesn't say which one. Her car is outside, so she must've called an ambulance. I'm so sorry I didn't come by earlier, Laila. I'm so sorry."

"Trey, calm down, honey. I'm at the hospital now."

"Okay. Okay, good."

"Come to Prince George's to be with me okay. She's on the maternity ward."

"She's in labor?"

"I guess so. Look, I'm getting off the elevator now, so call me when you get here."

The elevator doors face the maternity ward reception desk. Dr. Gray is leaning over the desk talking to a nurse when I step off the elevator. I stand quietly behind him, and patiently wait for him to finish his conversation. I am nervous, sweating from every pore on my body. The nurse he is talking to points at me.

He turns around and says, "Laila, I'm glad you're here. We're going to have to perform an emergency Caesarean on Tori. I have to go check on the OR, but I will be back in a moment to catch you up on everything."

"Okay, okay."

"Tori's in room 729, along with your friend."

"My friend?"

"Yes. I'm sorry...I don't remember her name right now." He points toward the room.

Wait, he said my friend. Is Christina here? Why is she here? Get over it, Laila. That's not important right now. I'm such a horrible person. I've stressed Tori out so much that she's gone into premature labor.

I take a deep breath, exhale, and let go of everything before walking into the room. Tori needs me right now, and I need to give her my undivided attention. I put a smile on my face, turn the knob on the door, and walk into the room.

As I enter the room, I loudly say, "Hey, baby." Then everything transitions into slow motion for a moment.

Tori says, "Hey," while repositioning herself in the bed. She looks at me for only a second, and then quickly looks across the room toward the TV. Following her head movement, I look that way, and see Nadia slowly lifting herself from the chair. I gasp and put my hand to my mouth. Quickly, I compose myself, drop my hand, and straighten my posture. I look back and forth between them, while fighting to hold back tears.

Softly, I ask, "Nadia, what are you doing here?"

She ignores my question. Instead, she says, "It was nice to meet you, Tori. I hope everything goes well, but I must be leaving now."

I whisper, "What's going on?"

Nadia grabs her things and walks out of the room. All I can do is stand there and look at the door.

My back is to Tori, so I can't see her face, but her tone is facetious when she says, "Go ahead. Go after her."

I take a deep breath, turn around, and look at her.

She says, "Baby, I'm serious. Go say goodbye to her."

"No, I'd better not."

"Laila, go."

I want to try to salvage something between us; Nadia is a true friend.

"Laila, GO!"

Tori's yelling makes me leave after Nadia. I casually walk to the door, and as soon as I close it behind me, I take off running down the hall. I catch Nadia just as she is about to get on the elevator. The elevator doors open, and she gestures for me to get on first. When the doors close, she hugs me. I am taken off guard.

"Nadia, I'm sorry. I didn't mean to hurt you."

"I know. I had a long talk with Tori. I wasn't expecting to find her at your house. 'Cause you told me she'd left you."

"I didn't mean for any of this to happen. I can explain."

"No, I don't want you to explain anything. It would be better if you just don't contact me for a couple of weeks so I can get over it because I am livid on the inside. I have an idea of what happened with Tori, but Camille is another story that may cause me to lose my mind on you. You played me like a fool."

"I know I've put us all in an uncomfortable predicament, Nadia, but—"

"Oh, you have done more than that, but don't worry about me. I'm good," she says sarcastically. "I won't let this interfere with our work relationship. But, just know I'm pissed off. You hear me? Pissed off."

"I would like to clear some things up about what happened."

"Laila, now is not the time. You need to get back to your fiancée and unborn child."

I rub my hands across my head and curse myself silently.

The elevator lands on the first floor, and the doors open just as I am about to say, "You're right. It's not, but I need to talk to you."

Nadia presses the button for the seventh floor, gets off the elevator, and blows me a kiss. Then she slowly walks away.

By the time I arrive back to Tori's room, they are ready to take her to the OR. Dr. Gray tells me they were waiting for me to come back, so I could see Tori before they took her to surgery. Hospital regulations no longer allow family members into the operating rooms, so I will have to wait here.

I go up to her and say, "Don't worry. Everything will be fine. I know things are crazy, but I love you with all my heart. Please believe that. I'm gonna fix everything."

She tells me, "I love you, too, and I still want to get married. So, everything has to be okay."

Tori is way too understanding right now. Something's not right. What went on with her and Nadia?

I smile at her and say, "Think of names for our baby boy."

"I will. All that really matters is our love. Tomorrow is a new day. Let's let all of this craziness go and start anew."

Dr. Gray and his team roll Tori away. I wave and say, "See you soon," as she disappears down the hallway.

I go into the room and think about how I ended up here, on the brink of losing everything. Shoot I still may. That fatal night I did not pay attention to, the night that spawned all of this, is haunting me. I wish I could rewind the clock. I have almost ruined everything. I hurt so many people, including myself, because I didn't take the time to ask questions. All those trumped up charges against her were totally off base. I've been toying with other people's lives and emotions because of my own selfish needs. I abandoned all that I knew and cared about because of a misconception, ain't that a bitch.

Tomorrow is a new day however, and I will work on getting back to the old me—the Laila Morriston I was before that night at the strip club, before that day at the harbor. Things will never be the same, but dammit, I'm gonna try to make them that way.

I just hope neither of these women tries to get back at me.

To be continued...

Every story has three sides! Stay tuned to hear what Laila's women have to say.

About the Author

Erika Renee Land is a native of Norfolk, Virginia. Upon graduating from high school, Erika enlisted in the United States Army, where she served for six and a half years.

In February 2009, Erika's military career ended, and she relocated to Athens, Georgia to attend the University of Georgia (UGA). Her initial plan was to attend pharmacy school; however, along the way, she discovered a hidden passion for writing and literature so she changed her major to English and embarked on a writing career.

During her academic transition, Erika found that writing is more than a passion. It also serves as a therapeutic tool, which helps her cope with Post Traumatic Stress Disorder stemming from her time spent supporting the war in Iraq. Erika also writes poetry, which can be found on her website: www.erikarland.com. The site also contains information on author appearances and much more.

Acknowledgments

Writing this book has been a long journey, and there have been many people who helped me accomplish publishing this book. Extending an encompassing thank you will not justify the gratitude I have for each of you, but to avoid leaving anyone out, I am compelled to write an all-inclusive 'Thank You.'

Family, friends, colleagues, associates, my publishing partners, and more: I want to thank you for your encouraging words, reads and re-reads, designs, edits, and so much more. Thank you for believing in me and my dreams. Thank you for providing direction for my ideas and spaces for them to flourish, as fly-by and random as they were at times. You all know who you are, so please accept this gracious THANK YOU.

To my mother, Renee Rhodes, there are not enough words. Without your love and guidance, *Misconceptions* may not have happened. Thank you for letting me know that as long as my decisions have merit, there will be light at the end of the tunnel.

I have love for you all.

ERL

Erika Renee Land

Coming Soon

IT'S
COMPLICATED

Book Two

Scorned

Introduction

I couldn't have imagined my first lesbian experience being like this. I'm on this elevator with a woman I thought loved me. She has deceived me gravely, but right now, while looking at her, I don't know what to do. A part of me wants to talk it out, find out what happened, because she can't be this malicious.

The first woman I've loved is not only engaged to another woman, but also is in love with someone else on top of that. She has three lovers that I know of, and I don't know where I fall on the pyramid.

I give it to her, though. Laila Morriston is a master of deception. I don't know what was and what wasn't true in our relationship. Laila made me feel amazing and seemed to be truthful. From the moment I met her, I took her to be extremely honest. Never did I think she was involved with someone else—or multiple people, for that matter. Talking to Victoria, her fiancée, only clarified a small portion of this mess for me. What goes around comes back around, though, and that's probably why she had to deal with Tasha stalking her ass. Thank goodness for that, because it probably wouldn't have come out that she is a...a...lying son of a bitch, yeah that's what she is. She likes to only tell half the story.

This is the second time someone has crushed my feelings. However, I won't be devastated like I was when my ex-husband Xavier didn't leave me a pot to piss in. Oh no, she will not get the best of me. I'm saying it now, Laila Morriston has scorned Nadia York, but she won't get away with it. She's not going to get off scott-free and go live happily ever after...especially since I have given myself to her sexually.

www.ingramcontent.com/pod-product-compliance
Lightning Source LLC
Chambersburg PA
CBHW072216170626
46813CB00003B/970